The Cabin

Synopsis

There is more to Rachel Clarke, the British born actress, than meets the eye…

In an effort to appear unavailable, and desperate to escape the advances of an admirer turned stalker, Rachel marries. But as the convenience wears off and exhaustion from filming sets in she finds herself seeking the refuge of her beloved cabin.

On her way an unexpected snowstorm throws her, literally, into the path of Jem with whom she forms a firm friendship; something she thought impossible with the 'tell-all' world of celebrity gossip. The easy going attitude in the small town of Bradely allows Rachel to let down her defences, in more ways than one.

Can Rachel finally find safety, security and love or will her she pay the ultimate price for her celebrity status?

Chapter 1

"Come with me if you want to live!" Rachel grabbed the large outstretched hand that hauled her effortlessly off the ledge of the burning building. The silky red dress she wore clung to her feminine curves, providing a glimpse of cleavage, while the fine material billowed around her shapely calves. He pulled her limp, submissive body against his chest and gave her a smouldering look with intensely blue eyes before reaching for her hand again.

He led her at speed through the narrow smoke filled corridor, a look of pure determination painting his strong masculine features. Rachel coughed against the back of her free hand before she was swept off her feet in one smooth motion, her petite frame cradled protectively against his chest. The buttons of his light blue, dirt smeared shirt were strategically undone, providing a tantalising glimpse of a muscular stomach and toned pecks which were dusted lightly with dark hair.

His long denim clad legs strode purposefully, slicing through the smoke causing it to swirl in patterns as it caught in the shafts of light beaming through the small square windows either side of them. As he approached the end of the corridor he turned his body and whipped his right leg up and out in a powerful karate kick, his size 12 boot making contact with the white door, snapping the lock, causing it to swing wildly on its hinges. The smoke dispersed and the light flooded in, framing their silhouetted figures in the doorway.

"And cut! Awesome guys!"

Matt gently lowered Rachel to the floor. Once her 3" heels touched terra firma she adjusted the flimsy material across her chest before running both hands down her legs to smooth the fly-away material. Sucking in a lungful of fresh air she raised her head, glanced across at the outrageously handsome co-star—who was biting nervously at a nail—before her gaze landed on a bespectacled, slightly plump man who was peering into a small shielded screen, nodding and talking quietly to a woman beside him.

Rachel waited pensively with her co-star, hands clasped tightly in front of her to prevent them from fiddling with her, currently, dark auburn wavy locks.

The Director leaned across in the opposite direction and exchanged words with another crew member, then after a quick study of another small screen, held in the hands of a lanky technician, he announced "Okay, let's break for lunch and be back at 2pm."

Matt blew out a breath he must have been holding and lowered his gaze to Rachel's. "Okay?"

Rachel surreptitiously rolled her shoulders and gave her limbs a shake as she stepped away from the hunk of maleness beside her. "Yeah, thanks. Great take Matt."

"You too. Want some lunch? Pete went to Maria's for some of those organic vegan boxes?"

"Errr." Rachel rummaged around her brain for a plausible excuse to escape but she was too pleasant for her own good.

"Come on!" He chuckled, which sounded more like a deep rumble than a laugh. "What could happen? It's not as if you can get food poisoning from that rabbit food!" Matt interjected.

"Exactly, rabbit food!" Rachel mumbled before she acquiesced, walking alongside Matt back to his trailer on the other side of the set. Her 5ft 7" was dwarfed by his 6ft 2" so she quickened her pace slightly to keep up with Matt's long legged stride, not an easy feat on the in the 3" stiletto heels across the changing surface which went from smooth dark tarmac to compacted gravel. "Why do you get those anyway?"

"Pete says it's good for me." He said as he shrugged his broad shoulders and gave her a lopsided smirk.

Rachel shook her head and let loose a gentle chuckle causing her long auburn hair to brush against her tanned bare shoulders, revealed by the low cut, off the shoulder deep red dress wardrobe had provided. They continued with the playful chatter as they made the relatively short walk across the set. Matt was so relaxed, with an easy humour that, even after a gruelling morning of re-takes, make-up and then a series of frustrating sound problems, which inevitably led to more re-takes, he could still make her smile.

As they journeyed to their Winnebago's some of the cast and set crew stopped to give a nod or a wave, before whispering to their co-workers. Honestly, those lot were the biggest load of gossips Rachel had ever met!

Matt gave her a sly sideways look before looping his arm over her shoulders and affixing the notoriously cheeky grin, which caused his lightly stubbled right cheek to dimple. She could see where his reputation as a Lothario came from, with gleaming white teeth and that dimple, framed with tussled dark hair; he was a ruggedly handsome guy who could no doubt get any girl he wanted.

However, they'd been working together now for two weeks and, to be fair to him, Matt had been a perfect gentleman. His sordid reputation seemed a million miles away from the gentle, if not cheeky, giant she knew. They had been getting along great, their easy banter on set had made this action movie more fun than Rachel had expected.

"After you." Matt put his hand on Rachel's lower back, nudging her up the metal steps to his trailer as he followed behind.

Matt's trailer was pretty much the same as hers, with a table and wrap around seating almost directly in front of the door as they entered, a compact kitchen to the left and small sitting area leading onto a bedroom and bathroom to the right. Pete, Matt's assistant, was pottering in the kitchen and welcomed them with a bright smile of his own as they entered.

"Hi guys, how'd it go?" Pete asked as he dried his hands on a brightly coloured plaid tea-towel, which he promptly flicked over his broad right shoulder. Like Matt he was tall, but instead of being stubbled, dimpled and tousled he was the epitome of precision; his strong jaw was closely shaven and his dark blond hair was styled into a tidy short back and sides with the longer hair on top combed and held in place by some invisible force, or fancy hair wax that couldn't be detected; unlike the glossy gel so many men opted for, inevitably making them look a bit greasy and, in Rachel opinion, sleazy.

"Great." Matt and Rachel said in unison as they plopped down at either end of the table.

Pete smiled and proceeded to place fancy looking take-out boxes of brightly coloured salad for each of them on the table. Rachel concentrated on her salad, spearing the cubes of beetroot, grated carrot and orange segments, trying desperately to avoid the kale. *'How does that fit in this bowl?!'*

Pete sat himself on a stool next to Matt. "So what's the next scene? Do you have a shoot this afternoon?"

Matt nodded as he shovelled a fork full of indiscriminate salad into his mouth. "Mmhhmm."

Pete gave him a half smile and raised a questioning eyebrow to Rachel, who swallowed purposefully and took a sip of cool water from the bottle in front of her before answering more coherently. "What he was saying is 'yes' we've got a final take this afternoon. We're doing the car stunt scene tomorrow, so we've got the room scene to do later." Rachel responded, waggling her eyebrows suggestively.

Pete nodded and focussed on his salad. "You ready for that one?"

Matt and Rachel looked at each other, the suggestive bravado from moments ago fading with the simple inquiry. "Yeah." Rachel swiped the napkin across her lips removing a trace of salad dressing and some of the deep red lipstick make-up had applied earlier. "You know now is as good a time as any. We haven't really talked about the love scenes. We could do with running through it before we get on set and everyone is watching us." Rachel continued.

In all honesty, they'd had no love scenes so far and she really didn't want that more intimate side of the story to impact on their easy-going, friendly relationship so far. In fact, she had no physical attraction to Matt; he felt more like a brother than a possible love interest. She just hoped he felt the same way and could be professional about it.

She'd had problems before with her on-scene love interests wanting to continue out of the limelight of the cameras, but inevitably it all ended up as tabloid gossip. The thoughts of being pursued by the press didn't appeal, especially when combined with the usually over-confident, self-absorbed stars she was generally paired with. Overall she found little attraction that was more than skin deep with her fellow actors, so had vowed against them. Her kind attempts at rejection however had varying levels of success, which at times, made shooting difficult.

Either way, with the mess of her life at the moment, she had no desire to pursue a relationship, especially when her libido was on the blink. In fact, she felt positively asexual. *'Why am I not attracted to anyone?'* Was a question she found swirling in her head more than once, it'd been 2 years now since her last relationship. Rachel pushed the thoughts aside and blamed it squarely on the recent stresses of her stalker and the uncomfortable feeling of being watched, not having her privacy and not feeling safe.

A flutter of anxiety began to swell in her chest, but before it could blossom into something more solid Matt interrupted, unknowingly quelling the probable panic attack that lurked when thoughts of Mark Copland invaded her consciousness.

"Yeah." Matt said distractedly, seemingly deep in thought himself, but it broke Rachel away from her own internal dialogue and it took a moment to remember what they were discussing. Matt clarified it for her. "Let's finish eating and we can run through the lines."

"Right." Rachel speared a raspberry, gave it a curious look before showing more determination to consume the healthy, if not bizarre, concoction that was her lunch.

Once they had finished eating, well Matt shovelling and Rachel picking, they had an hour to run through the scene. "I know Andre really wants this scene to be hot and heavy so we're gonna have to really lay it on." Matt said distractedly while he perused the script, his unbelievably blue eyes dancing over the page as he read.

"Okay." Rachel concentrated on the script and the plethora of notes she had scrawled during the meeting with Andre, their director. Suddenly the small trailer seemed to crackle with tension as the pair prepared, shaking themselves loose and chuckling at the awkwardness as they transformed themselves back into the professionals they were.

"You could have died out there!" Matt growled, grabbing Rachel by her upper arms and thrust her against the hard plains of his chest.

"Ooof" Rachel panted, immediately reaching up to lay both her palms flat on Matt's chest so that she could plant her feet more solidly on the thick carpet and push away from the solid wall of muscle in order to generate a little distance. "Sorry…you knocked the wind out of me, can we do that again?"

Matt repositioned and then paced back to his mark. "You could have died out there!" Matt growled, again taking Rachel by her upper arms and pulling her, not quite as hard, against himself. He leaned his head down and kissed her roughly before Rachel pushed him away, again positioning both hands flat against his chest. He stumbled a few steps back and Rachel paused for a moment before surging forward, hands either side of his toned stomach, drawing the audiences eye to the well-defined six pack revealed by the open shirt he wore, and reached up to kiss him again. Matt took her face between his large palms to strategically angle her face for the camera and returned what appeared to be a heated kiss.

After a beat or two Rachel pulled away. "Okay, we're gonna need a step or platform. The height difference I think is going to be a problem." Rachel said, her professional demeanour seemingly at odds with the scene that they had just enacted. Internally she dismissed another leading man, '*not even remotely affected by the kiss…an urrgghh stubble!*' she thought as she unconsciously tugged at her chin.

✳✳✳

On set the scene went without any major hitches and they managed to bag it without too many re-do's. According to the crew it 'smouldered', only fuelling the gossip about their off-screen relationship, which inevitably leaked to the media.

Over the next few days a multitude of grainy images of the pair on set, arm in arm, Matt touching Rachel's lower back and going into each other's trailer could be found on the Internet, trashy talk shows and various magazines. Rachel flung the gossip rag onto the pale wooden coffee table in her trailer. To be honest she wasn't bothered, they were both free and single, so there were no names being dragged through the mud.

Rachel's inner musings were disturbed by a sharp tap, followed by a ruffle of dark hair that belonged to Matt, as he peeped his head around the unlocked door.

"Hi Rach. Are you busy?"

"Nah! Just having a breather. Have you seen this?" Rachel pointed at the magazine in front of her.

"Yeah…about that, can we talk?"

"Mmhhmm." She answered absently as she shuffled over to make space for Matt's huge frame, tucking her bare feet up underneath herself as she did.

Matt stepped in and shut the door firmly behind him before folding himself into the space next to Rachel on the faux leather sofa. He looked slightly agitated, his hands were running up and down his denim clad thighs and his gaze went to the door several times before he finally let out a deep breath and turned himself to face Rachel more fully.

"Everything okay Matt?" Rachel was perplexed but affixed a mask of politeness to hide her curiosity. Another loud exhalation exploded from Matt before he looked Rachel in the eye and took one of her hands in his. Rachel gulped, her stomach hitting the floor. *'Gees I hope this is not a proposition; he's like my brother…okay a weird one who I snog on set, but urghhh!'*

"Okay, here's the thing…" Matt let out another breath and Rachel could see the sweat beading on his brow and his complexion had turned a light shade of green.

"Bloody hell Matt, are you okay? Do you need a glass of water or something?" Rachel's American accent slipped into her native British, something she was trying to avoid while she played an American in this movie. She moved to stand, but Matt kept a firm grasp of her hand.

"NO!…Sorry, I just need to say this" He tugged Rachel back into place on the sofa before he continued. "…okay…so, virtually nobody knows this about me…" More deep breathing ensued and Rachel rubbed Matt's forearm reassuringly. "Okay, so here goes…" Another long pause followed until Matt finally finished. "I'm gay." Matt sat stock still watching Rachel carefully.

Rachel broke a smile. "Phew, I thought you were going ask me out or something!"

Matt chuckled and then laughed. "Maybe I am!"

"Huh?"

Chapter 2

4 Years later…

Rachel heaved a large brown leather carry-on bag up her shoulder and tugged at the handle of the hefty suitcase, which wobbled precariously behind her as she exited the quiet airport terminal and crossed the road to where her SUV was parked. The cold afternoon air caused a shiver and sharp intake of breath that left her lungs tingling.

As she walked she fumbled with her phone one handedly, eventually succeeded in turning it on—the welcome notes echoing noisily off the concrete walls that made up the long stay parking bays. Rachel deftly fired off a quick text to Matt, Mum and Sarah as she approached her SUV in the virtually deserted parking facility; environments like this always made her feel anxious and she sped up, going as fast as she could without causing the little wheels on the bulbous suitcase to lose their battle with balance.

Rachel shoved the phone back into the pocket of her warm ski jacket and dug a little deeper into the oversized space to retrieve the keys.

Thankful to be nearing her end destination she unceremoniously shoved the suitcase onto the back seat and huffed her frustration as she rifled through the shoulder bag to extract her black leather Mulberry handbag.

Finally free of the cumbersome baggage Rachel suddenly felt weightless as she hopped into the beloved midnight blue Jeep Patriot, the cold leather sending a jolt of surprise through her body. *'I'm too used to LA'* Rachel thought as she adjusted the scarf and rummaged in yet another pocket of the ski jacket for her woolly hat.

Once all her extra layers were in place she rubbed her fingers together and twisted the ignition key, the Jeep roared into life on the first attempt and she lovingly caressed the steering wheel. "Good boy!" It wasn't fancy or new but the Jeep was the first American car she had bought, along with her cabin, therefore it had a special place in her heart.

As Rachel made the hour long drive to Kolton—the nearest large town from Bradely where her cabin was situated—she smiled broadly. *'No more filming or publicity, just me, relaxing at the cabin, painting and, thank goodness, sleeping.'* She was exhausted, but after a moment of procrastination decided that making the detour to the supermarket now would mean she could stay in bed for at least the next 2 days without having to go out looking for sustenance.

The actress pulled into the vast car park, littered with the odd stray trolley and found a parking space not too far from the main entrance. After killing the ignition she pulled down the visor and flipped open the small mirror, casting a critical eye over her appearance. She tugged the hat lower and tucked in a few loose blonde strands. *'No-one will recognise me like this, hopefully.'*

As an A-list celebrity she was often recognised, it was inevitable. She'd been working pretty much non-stop for the past 3 years so she had more than covered her quota of box office hits and advertising bill boards. Rachel was her publicists dream, but even she was encouraging Rachel to get away and take a break.

Once she was all stocked up on food and necessities Rachel made the final leg of the journey to Bradely, her home from home for the next few months at least. As she travelled along the freeway the concrete and tarmac of the urban area morphed into open fields, then scattered woodland with steep mountainsides and grey rocky escarpments. As she drove the snow began to flurry around her, turning the lush countryside a fresh shade of white and eventually deepening as the vehicle wound its way further and climbed higher into the mountains.

Upon reaching Bradely she could feel a 'calm' wash over her. It felt safe, it felt like home. There were no eyes on her, no uncomfortable sensations of being followed and no unhappy memories of *him*. Rachel shuddered involuntarily and then chastised herself for allowing her calm to be suddenly overshadowed by a past that had not happened here in this sheltered little town.

After taking a right at the only junction in Bradely she spotted the red and green painted shop front. With a raised, covered wooden walkway and hanging sign it reminded her of the old American wild west movies she used to watch as a kid, a thought that always caused a wave of nostalgia to pass over her as she fondly recollected her childhood in the Yorkshire Dales, a place that seemed so far away, like it was in another lifetime, but yet like it was just yesterday at the same time. *'How weird.'*

The small community and relatively unmodernised Main Street were what had attracted Rachel to this town in the first place and it hadn't disappointed. Even when the residents realised they had a celebrity in their midst they rarely gave her a second look and over the years, despite keeping herself to herself, she still felt accepted.

Rachel pulled to a stop behind a red, weather beaten SUV in front of the store which belonged to Lucy, a rather tenacious lady who must be well into her 70's, if not 80's by now. Her hair was as white as the driven snow and her face spoke of a life of laughter, written in every wrinkle and crease around her mouth and eyes. As they would say in Yorkshire, Lucy called a 'spade' a 'spade'. In other words she never minced her words, but once she grew to like you she was fiercely protective and an excellent ally, and no

14

doubt terrifying foe. Although Rachel had never once heard a bad word spoken against her.

Since Rachel had bought the cabin from her 10 years previously, Lucy had always taken care of it while she was away and would get in a few essentials and chase out the cold with a fire when she knew Rachel was making her trek from 'the big smoke', as Lucy liked to call it.

As it was, Lucy knew she was travelling today and no matter how tired Rachel was it would be unforgivable to drive by without checking in. Plus the snow was really falling now, and despite owning the cabin for the last 10 years, she'd rarely visit in the winter. *'Maybe Mike could fit those snow chains Lucy insisted I buy.'* She thought hopefully.

The store was like a throwback from the 1950's, it stocked everything from bread to motor oil, magazines to ski wear and locally made knits and alcohol. The stuff in it wasn't old or outdated, but the sheer diversity, tightly crammed onto shelves and rails reminded her of days gone by, before the big superstores had driven shops like these out of business.

On arrival Lucy gave Rachel a warm hug and introduced her to Jem, her Granddaughter who was laughing with another older lady and eying a bottle of deep burgundy liquid suspiciously. Jem and Rachel exchanged polite handshakes as Lucy gushed about Jem's credentials as a paramedic and ski instructor in the winter months. Jem's long brown hair was swept up into a messy bun and her cheeks reddened as Lucy boasted about her.

"Enough Gram!" Jem held her hands up, as if in surrender. "I've got to go up to the hotel and check on the bookings. Now the snow is coming down I might get some early lessons in." Jem gave Lucy an affectionate squeeze before hastily exiting the shop, the bell on the front door tinkling as it swung shut.

Lucy and Rachel fell into the easy conversation of people who had been acquainted for years. It was this kind of normality that life in LA couldn't provide, making Bradely her sanctuary.

By the time Rachel left, to traverse the last part of the journey up to the cabin, Lucy had sold her the suspicious bottle of homebrew – alcoholic content unknown – and a jar of her own homemade chutney, complete with a square of red and white gingham cloth and a ribbon to hold it in place over the lid.

As she stepped out onto the street the snow swirled. It looked like a snow globe that had just been shaken, beautiful but frantic.

"Hey Mike, can you put the snow chains on Rachel's truck?" Lucy hollered behind Rachel, causing her to jump and then juggle to the contents in her arms to avoid dropping them.

"It's okay, the Jeep should be fine." Rachel returned, not wanting to put Mike out, but secretly hoping he would insist. Mike was Lucy's Grandson whom she'd met pretty much every time she visited. He was fairly tall, about 6ft with a muscular frame, strong jaw and the same soft, caring brown eyes as Lucy, and as she now knew, Jem too.

Mike emerged from behind his own truck, wearing a fleece lined deer stalker. "Hi Rachel, how are you?" He had a warm smile that crinkled his eyes, reminding her again of his dear Grandmother.

"I'm fine Mike. How about you? Rita good?"

"Yeah." His smile grew wider. "We're havin' a baby!"

"Oh, congratulations, that's fantastic news." Rachel looked down at her arms, which were full, and lent forward to give Mike a half hug, which he accepted warmly.

Lucy interrupted the pleasantries. "Can you put some snow chains on Rachel's truck? I think she'll need them to get up the track now."

"No problem, I'll do it now." Mike gave Rachel a quick nod before adding. "It'll only take 5, but you'll be glad of them."

"Thanks, but only if you have time though?"

"Of course. No problem." '*Phew.*'

Chapter 3

Large fat snowflakes floated and then zoomed as they splatted against the windscreen, the wipers frantically scraping across the glass in a battle against the onslaught of snow. The situation had rapidly escalated to a full on 'white-out' which left Rachel crawling up the mountain at a paltry speed.

With each passing minute the snow was getting deeper and deeper, causing an unsettled flutter of panic in her chest. The poor visibility made it impossible to work out where she was, despite the fact that she had owned the cabin for the last decade and had made this journey thousands of times.

Eventually the large rock and the turning sign, where the track for her cabin peeled off from the highway suddenly came into view, just a blur against the snow that swirled around her. Rachel had to react quickly to make the turning, causing the SUV to skid, its back end momentarily lost grip and swung 45° in the road. Rachel gritted her teeth and clung to the steering wheel so tightly her knuckles were white, but kept her cool as she gently touched the gas and brought the 4 x 4 back under control before making the gentle incline up the windy track to her beloved getaway.

The gravel and dirt track was heavily laid with snow that made a gentle swishing noise as the large chain clad tyres broke the pristine surface. Everything was eerily silent other than the swishing and crunching of the snow and the staccato breathing of the anxious actress at the wheel.

"Not far now and we'll be home bud." She gently reassured herself and the SUV as they navigated the winding track. The flurries of snow continued to bombard the windshield. The wooded area around them was bright white from the blanket of fresh snow and stumps of brown were all that could be seen of the large pines, their branches already burgeoning from the weight of the accumulation upon them.

Her SUV slowed, the swishing becoming more of a groan, as the snow deepened at an opening in the woods where there was a steep hollow off to one side. In the summer it was beautiful, the concave bowl of earth was surrounded by trees with a stream that fed into a small creek at the bottom. Often she would simply sit and watch the fish and wildlife that visited to lap its clear waters. However, this afternoon there were no animals and no burbling brook, just the groan and creak of the overworked engine. The wheels jammed and then spun wildly as she pressed the gas, even the chains on the tyres were failing to grip onto the soft powdery snow.

"Damn it!"

Leaving the engine running and the lights on full beam, Rachel began twisting and rummaging in the back foot-well amongst the bags until she laid her hands on the cold steel of the snow shovel. Taking a deep breath she heaved it free, smacking herself in the chin with the wooden handle as she did.

"Fuck, shit, bollocks….arghhh." She rubbed her chin furiously as her eyes watered. "Bloody typical me." Her hands stilled on her chin and a resigned sigh crossed her lips. "Urgh, can't I just be there already?"

Reaching across to the passenger seat, careful not to whack herself with the shovel, again, she grabbed her fleece lined ski gloves and tugged them on. She took another steadying breath while mentally preparing herself for the cold she was about to leap into. She heaved the door open and jumped into the snow, surprised at how deep it actually was. The icy wind felt like a slap in the face as she rounded the car and began shovelling the snow from around the tyres. Despite the freezing conditions she could feel her face flush with effort and a fine sheen of sweat formed on the back of her neck which, with the rhythmic shovelling, was intermittently exposed to the arctic air, sending a shiver down her spine. It was a strange combination of heat and cold that made her feel feverish.

 "I'd rather be in the hot tub." She shouted loudly into the surroundings as she continued to heave the snow with the short shovel. The muscles in her arms, thighs and lower back burned and protested as she dug out the final tyre. Once clear of snow she wiped her face with a cold, snow encrusted glove before throwing the shovel back into the foot well with a burst of enthusiasm she didn't really feel. She hoicked open her door and slumped herself back into the driver seat, her face still flushed from the exertion of shovelling the deep snow.

 "Right truck, let's get this show on the road."

 The engine was still running and the car felt stiflingly hot as Rachel found the biting point and gently lifted the clutch and pushed the accelerator. The car began pulling forward and after a beat Rachel roughly grabbed her hat and threw it onto the passenger seat as a wave of dizziness struck her from the rapid temperature change. This momentary waver in concentration was all it took for the clutch peddle to slip and the car lurched to the left. As if in slow motion it began to slide from the track, veering at an unnatural angle as it descended sideways down the slope into the hollow below. Rachel braced herself as eerily slowly, yet too fast to react, she saw the crash unfolding. A large pine tree careered ever closer, instinct made her shut her eyes and brace for the impact. A long drawn out shriek echoed through the darkening surrounds until the air was knocked from her lungs and any noise she made was drowned by the sound of crushing metal, the smashing of glass and the dull thud of her head against the side of the car. As Rachel blinked her eyes open the silence was overwhelming and her vision blurred.

Jem peered out from her crouching position by the battered snow mobile, wiping her hands on an old rag as she hollered across the garage into the shop.

"Hey Gram, do you have any spray oil?"

"Hmmm"

Jem tried again, calling out a little louder "I said, do you have…"

"I heard you" Lucy interrupted testily. "It's been 2 hours and I still haven't heard a peep from Rachel. I just buzzed her on the CB and she's not responding."

The worry caused the heavily ploughed furrows on Lucy's face to deepen as she stood, hands on hips, staring at the CB radio, presumably willing it to speak to her.

"I don't like it. Jem, please will you take Bobby and check that she's not stuck on the track. The snow has been coming on stronger than Rick when you wore that dress at the ski dance last year."

Jem frowned, remembering Rick's none too subtle come on's and persistence on the dance floor that made her more than a little uncomfortable. Jem shook her head at her grandmother before grabbing the can of spray oil she held out for her. "Grammmm" She half moaned and half chastised before registering the level of worry across the old lady's features. "Ok, no worries, I'll check." She finished spraying a nut on the snow mobiles engine and then grabbed her gloves and scarf from the side. "I'll radio you when I get there, she might have just forgotten."

21

Her attempt at reassurance just caused Lucy to shake her head. "No, Rachel wouldn't forget. She's not that kind of girl."

"Are you sure Gram? These celebrity types seem to be a bit self-involved. She might have other stuff on her mind."

"Why would you say that? You've never even met her before. You know what they say about books and covers and what-not and well you remember that young lady."

Jem sighed softly, she hadn't meant to be judgemental. "I'm just saying…look, she's been in the magazines a lot lately."

"I know, apparently getting a divorce. I never saw that boy here once. God only knows why she married him. She adores this place so much you'd have thought she'd want to share it with someone she really loves." Lucy gave Jem a knowing look before shooing her onto Bobby, the snow mobile, and patting her gently on the shoulder and kissing her lovingly on the helmet as she buckled the strap under her chin. "Go steady now and don't forget to radio when you get there."

The snow mobile hummed into life after a short stutter and Jem manoeuvred up the hill to take the shortcut through the woods. The cold air whipped her face causing her to adjust the scarf so it covered any exposed skin below her goggles. Her breath warmed the fleecy material and the clean smell of laundry detergent mixed with the fresh air reminded her of the winters spent at the mountain with her Gram and the on-coming ski season that she loved so much.

The snow mobile made good time on the newly laid snow, skimming lightly across its surface, making a wake behind her as she ploughed on through into the woods. The snow storm had eased, dramatically improving visibility. The whole area looked brand new, a perfect winter wonderland. If the snow was anything to go by this seasons skiing would be some of the best.

As she approached the log cabin a swirl of dark smoke could be seen curling from the chimney. Jem shook her head. "She did forget." She muttered to herself softly. However, as she rounded to the front of the cabin she couldn't see Rachel's SUV and, as dusk was approaching, no lights were on and all the snow was pristine.

"Huh, Gram's fire must still be going." Jem felt a twinge of remorse and she quietly chastised herself for making a judgment based on the chatter of gossip magazines.

She steered Bobby down the track and flicked on the headlights to illuminate the darkening path as it led into the woods. Jem gave an involuntary shiver at the prospect of the dark and cold, but steeled herself and continued to make her way into the copse where the large pines loomed tall and mighty. Halfway down the snow covered track she could see disturbances in the snow and had to stand up on the foot rails and lean across carefully to look down the slope into the hollow below.

"Shit!"

The SUV was resting on a tree partially down the incline. There were no lights, no engine, no sound, just the ragged noise of her own breathing against the scarf covering her nose and mouth.

"Shit…Rachel?…Rachel, can you hear me?….Are you there?" She paused, listening intently, but again the only sounds she could make out were her own stilted breaths and the whoosh of blood pulsing in her eardrums. Paramedic training kicked in as she hopped off Bobby and cautiously slid, digging the heels of her snow boots in to slow her descent down to the car, which was leant against a large pine. Peering through the open passenger door she could see the smashed glass and crushed door, but the vehicle was empty. She began calling out again and frantically scanning the area around the car. *'Maybe she went back down the track…that would make sense.'* As Jem started to climb the slope she saw a huddled figure in the snow. At first the black jacket and white ski pants looked like a rock in the dimming light, but on second glance she could make out the black stripe down the outside seam and a flash of pink from Rachel's snow boots. Jem made short work of getting to Rachel, despite the deep snow, which made her breathless as she fell to her knees next to the figure.

"Rachel?"

Rachel turned her head and gave a glassy eyed look at the masked figure in front of her.

Pulling down the scarf and quickly propping the goggles on top of her black helmet Jem quickly scanned Rachel's face before making eye contact. "Rachel, it's Jem. Lucy sent me to check on you. What happened?" *'Duh, like that wasn't obvious.'* Jem suppressed the desire to roll her eyes at herself and remained focussed on the intensely blue eyes staring back at her.

"Bloody snow! Car went off the track…banged my head." She weakly held a gloved hand to her left temple.

"Anywhere else hurt?" Jem gently probed.

"No, just cold. Tried to get to the cabin, but it's just too deep."

Jem gently patted Rachel down, checking for any obvious pain points, before rising to her feet and holding out her hands to help Rachel up. "Come on; let's get you home and warm."

Rachel nodded and grasped Jem's hands as she stumbled to her feet, groaning, before looking Jem with a little more awareness and quietly thanked her. With arms linked around each other they made their way back up the slope where, after helping Rachel onto the back of the snow mobile, Jem snuck in front and held Rachel's hands with one of her own across her middle. "Hold on, okay?"

"Okay." It was barely a whisper as Rachel leaned into Jem's back, her head snuggled against the warm shoulder as she failed to hold her heavy head up as the snowmobile jostled and struggled up the incline. Rachel could just about feel Jem's muscles flexing through her thick jacket as she steered back up the snowy track. In just 5 minutes they were back at the cabin and again, arm in arm, made it up the steps into the comfortable warmth of the cabin. Jem led Rachel to the couch and helped her to sit before quickly throwing off her gloves and helmet. She stoked the fire and threw on a couple of logs before turning to assess the celebrity on the couch. Jem knelt in front of Rachel and removed her hat while casting her eyes over the familiar face in front of her.

"You okay?"

Rachel simply nodded, before seemingly rousing herself. "Yeah, just a bit cold." She said before peeling her hands out of her thick gloves. Jem gave Rachel another assessing look, then after a beat, stood and whirled into action. Rachel observed from the couch, still in a daze from the cold and no doubt the bang on her head. Jem filled and put the kettle on the stove before reaching for the CB on the counter by the door.

"'Puddle Duck' to 'Old Woman', do you read me?" Rachel raised her lips in a crooked smile that made Jem smile and shrug at the quirky call signs.

"Jem, thank God. Everything ok?"

"Yep, we're safe…Rachel got stuck in the snow and was walking up." Rachel raised an eyebrow at Jem who quickly turned to study the device in front of her. "That's why it took so long. The snow is real deep here."

"You all okay?"

"Fine, just getting warmed up. I'm gonna stay though, it's getting dark, but I'll be back down in the morning, okay?"

"Sounds good, I don't want you driving Bobby back down tonight. Take care of each other. Over and out."

"Good night 'Old Woman', over and out."

"Less of that 'Puddle Duck'. Out."

As Jem returned the receiver to the hook Rachel laughed. "I think you just got told off, Puddle Duck!"

Jem chuckled, "Yeah, never too old to get told by Gram."

"I take it you're staying?"

"Yes. It's dark and you've had a bump to the head. It's safer all round."

"Right, that's very authoritative of you!" Rachel chuckled to soften the comment, before adding "Thanks for not broadcasting that I can't drive in the snow and crashed my car! It's hard enough shaking the media image without adding my own stupidity to the mix."

Jem simply nodded in acknowledgement and began filling 2 large mugs with hot water as the kettle whistled loudly on the stove. Before she could deliver the steaming cups of tea she realised that she had left a watery path as the snow from her boots melted in the warm cabin. Approaching the back door, between the kitchen and the fireplace, she kicked off her snow boots, stripped off the ski jacket and then shimmied out of her salopettes, hanging them on the plethora of hooks attached to the side of the warm stone chimney breast. Grabbing the cups she padded back across the room to the living area and placed them on the rustic oak coffee table in front of Rachel and the fire.

"Thanks" Rachel blew the steam from the hot tea and took a tentative sip.

Jem watched, momentarily mesmerised by Rachel's familiar full lips and straight nose. *'It's weird seeing a celebrity in real life!'* A hint of blush pinked her cheeks when she realising she was staring and so she covered her tracks by taking a large gulp of tea, inadvertently scolding her tongue. After a few more sips Jem broke the silence. "You should get out of your outdoor clothes and I can check out that bump on your head…do you remember that I'm a paramedic in the off season?"

Rachel nodded as she set the cup on the table and began unfastening her jacket. As Rachel fought her arms out of the sleeves she twisted and then clutched at her left side. "Arrghh, beast!" She roared.

At the deep rumbling groan, which seemed like an unexpected noise from Rachel, Jem immediately put down her cup and rushed to her side. "What's up? Are you hurt?"

"I must have banged my side when I hit the tree." She winced.

"Okay, steady. Let me help." Jem eased Rachel's arms carefully from her jacket and dropped it to the floor. "Where does it hurt?"

Rachel gently laid her hands onto her left side where her ribs were and Jem sat down on the coffee table in front of her. "Okay, can I have a look and check out the damage? Bruised ribs can be really sore, but we need to check for breakages, they can cause other problems."

Jem's tone was soothing yet authoritative and Rachel instantly felt reassured, so she nodded before adding "Okay. Do you need me to take my sweater off?"

"How about I help you, I don't want you to hurt yourself again!" She raised her eyebrow at Rachel who gave a soft chuckle before wincing at the sharp pain that shot across her side.

"How did I not notice this before? It bloody kills!"

Jem chuckled again, Rachel had an interesting way with words which highlighted her British accent. As she reached for the hem of Rachel's sweater she looked her in the eye. "Okay? Can you raise your arms and I'll pull your jumper over your head." Rachel simply nodded while she registered the rich chocolate of Jem's eyes and the crinkle of worry that caused little 'v' lines across the middle of her forehead. Seeing her up close Rachel could really note the family resemblance between her and Lucy, a familiarity that made her instantly more at ease. As the jumper lifted so did her vest, revealing a lightly tanned and toned tummy, which Jem quickly covered by pulling the vest back down with one hand before proceeding to lift the sweater over Rachel's head with the other. Once free of Rachel's hair Jem placed the sweater next to her on the stylishly faded and lightly battered leather couch. Rachel lifted the vest to reveal her stomach once again. "How does it look?"

Jem scanned her stomach before gently touching Rachel's hand. "Do you mind if this comes off too?"

"No, that's okay." As Jem removed the vest her warm hands brushed across Rachel's torso making her shiver.

"Sorry, are my hands cold?"

"No, it's just me being silly. How do they look?"

"Mmmm, I'm just going to put on some pressure. It might hurt, but I'm just feeling each rib to see if there are any obvious fractures." Jem gently but firmly palpated each rib while Rachel bowed her head to watch the gentle probing and the look of quiet concentration on Jem's face. After a couple of minutes Jem seemed happy with her examination, apart from the occasional squeak from Rachel they didn't seem too bad. "I think they're gonna go a lovely colour over the next day or two, but as far as I can see they're just bruised. If they don't start easing up or you get any sudden and sharp pain, that seems a lot worse than usual, then you should go to the hospital and get an x-ray."

"Thank you Doctor."

"Errr, I think you just promoted me beyond my station. It's Paramedic Jemima Shaw." Jem held out her hand as a formal introduction.

"Well, thank you Paramedic Shaw for your assessment." Rachel took her hand and gave it a firm shake.

"You're welcome Ms Clarke."

"Well now the official formalities are over I think I'd better find some clothes."

Suddenly aware of Rachel's lack of top Jem blushed and averted her eyes from the golden, flawless skin and simple white t-shirt bra.

"Of course." Was all Jem could come up with as Rachel made her way out of the living area, along the honey coloured hardwood flooring to the bedroom at the back of the cabin, her boots causing a slight echo through the hallway as she went. Jem busied herself, drinking the now tepid tea and loading another log onto the fire, before pushing her slender fingers through the mane of tousled brown hair in a vain attempt to make herself look more respectable. After gazing into the fire she realised Rachel had been gone nearly 10 minutes, worried she padded down the hallway to the bedroom door. "Rachel, how are you doing? Need any help?"

"I'm so sorry, I feel completely useless." She said through the door, and after a moment added. "You can come in." Jem pushed open the door and stood uneasily in the entrance. "Please could you help me? I can't get these damn boots off. Every time I bend down my ribs hurt like hell."

"Stop apologising…you had a nasty bump out there." Jem strode across the room and knelt at Rachel's feet and tugged off the snow boots. "Do you want some help with the salopettes too?"

"Ermmmm." Rachel looked skywards, feeling a little awkward at the damsel in distress she had seemingly become in the last hour or so, especially in front of someone new. Rachel couldn't stop her stream of self-deprecating thoughts. *What on Earth must she think of me, honestly, I'm so lame.* Rachel bowed and shook her head before looking at the bowed figure in front of her. "Please." Rachel popped the button of the padded ski pants and Jem tugged the hem from her kneeling position, pulling them down to reveal a pair of shapely legs encased in black leggings. "You know, I'm normally a very independent woman, none of this celebrity diva stuff people keep writing about."

"Hey, stop." Jem held up her hands in a gesture of surrender, she could clearly see the regret and worry in celebrity's eyes. "My Gram taught me not to judge a book by its cover, so stop panicking about what the newspapers say. To be honest I don't read celebrity gossip anyway." *Okay, that's a white lie, but it's only a little one for the greater good.* "No offence, but there are more important things to me than which celeb is dating who, or how many pounds they've put on this week!...And before you say it" Jem looked Rachel in the eye "stop with the apologies and thank you's." At that Jem stood, salopettes still in hand and left the bedroom, leaving Rachel sat on the bed looking at her feet.

Rachel appeared 5 minutes later wearing a thick woollen sweater that ended mid-thigh over her black leggings, the aromas from the kitchen drawing her to the stove where Jem stood stirring a pan.

"That smells good."

"It's just some chicken soup from the cupboard. I hope you don't mind, but I was hungry and figured you probably were too."

"Yeah definitely. The bread is in the car. Will bread sticks do?" Rachel said as she rummaged in the full length pull out pantry cupboard that was bursting with tins, bottles of herbs and an array of cereals in gaudy coloured boxes.

As Jem concentrated on the soup Rachel busied herself setting the table. Once Jem had decanted the soup into the chunky earthenware bowls they sat opposite each other at the small rustic oak table that matched the coffee table, situated in-between the kitchen and lounge.

"Candles huh?" Jem raised her shapely eyebrows at Rachel.

"Extra heat." Rachel said deadpan as she raised a spoon of steaming soup to her lips. After taking a sip Rachel looked up and couldn't hold her face straight any longer as she took in the curiously perplexed look that held Jem's features.

Rachel cracked one of her award winning smiles and Jem simply blinked, in awe of the perfect white teeth and genuine smile that reached Rachel's eyes, before she began laughing herself. '*What's so funny, she had no idea, but couldn't help herself, Rachel's laughter was infectious.*'

After that ice breaker the conversation flowed easily, discussing Rachel's summers, Jem's winters and childhood up here on the mountain. It turned out that every year they must have pretty much passed each other on the road, one coming and the other going. It was a miracle they had never met before today.

After the dishes were all washed and put away the girls curled themselves up at opposite ends of the couch holding onto tumblers of schnapps, the fire crackled and they both lost themselves in the hypnotising dance of the amber flames. After a while Jem tore her gaze from the fire and took in Rachel's profile. She really was beautiful; well defined eyebrows, perfectly plucked of course, a well-proportioned straight nose and plump lips that shimmered with moisture from the apricot schnapps, not a trace of make-up could be detected. Her hair fell in soft blond waves down to her shoulder blades and was tucked delicately behind her left ear. As her eyes roamed over Rachel's hair she noticed a hint of red peeking through the hairline. Jem placed her tumbler on the coffee table and reached across to part the fair hair and get a better look at the wound. Rachel seemed surprised by the action and gingerly recoiled from Jem's touch, her ribs still protesting despite taking some pain relief tablets earlier.

"Er, what you doin' Jem?"

"Hold still a moment. You banged your head didn't you?"

"Yeah, when I hit that bloody tree…I forgot about that."

Jem's fingers gently smoothed away Rachel's hair and she leant forward to get a good look at the damage. Rachel could feel Jem's warm breath on her ear and the gentle caress of her hair made her sigh. *'When was the last time someone touch me with such care? And for a minute I nearly freaked out thinking she was some weirdo fan.'* Realising what she'd done her cheeks pinked with a slight blush and she let out another shaky breath.

"Sorry…does that hurt?"

"Just a little." she said to cover her reaction to Jem's caring touch. "But it's fine."

Jem smoothed Rachel's hair one last time, enjoying the softness and floral scent from her shampoo. *'I wonder what brand she uses?'* She shook her head and quietly scolded herself for being star-struck. "You've got a bit of a bump and a bruise coming through but it looks okay. If you have any blurring, dizziness, loss of vision or bad headache you'd best get it checked out."

Rachel gently retraced the path of Jem's fingers, still feeling the slight tingle from her careful scrutiny and nodded. As the evening wore on the girls sat in companionable silence while they snuggled into the soft overstuff cushions of the sofa, listening to the fire crackle until the embers burnt low. The howling of the wind outside seemed to wake them from their reverie and Rachel shivered. Jem gave her an assessing look. "I think you should go to bed. It's late and you've had a busy day. How are you feeling?"

"To be honest a bit tired and sore, but nothing unexpected."

"Right, to bed with you. Do you have any blankets? I'll sleep on the sofa." Rachel's cabin was small and cosy. From helping her Gram stock up she knew it only had 1 bedroom, but it did have a long galley gym, office and a small hot tub on the wrap around porch.

Rachel chewed her lower lip and folded her arms across her chest. "I'm really sorry, I don't. The spares are in the car, I decided to wash them after my sister brought her kids and the puppy with her last time." Suddenly Rachel rose to her feet and looked at Jem. "It's a queen sized bed, we'll just have to share. It's too cold for you to sleep on the sofa with just a thin blanket…it's the least I can do for you after all of your chivalrous-ness! Is that even a word? Well, you know what I mean…Or I can take the sofa, I don't mind." Rachel rambled.

"I thought you said it was too cold for me on the sofa?" Jem replied as she got up from the sofa and stood in front of Rachel.

Rachel was slightly taller, but not by much and the two women stood, arms crossed over their chests, facing each other.

"Well whatever, I don't mind." Rachel shrugged. "Like I said, it's the least I can do after all of your help. If you hadn't come I probably would have spent all night out in the snow, and well, we know that wouldn't have ended well." Rachel held Jem's gaze before looking down and tapping her socked toes on the wooden floor.

'God she's adorable.' Jem shook the thought "Well, if you don't mind sharing I don't mind either."

With that Rachel headed from the lounge towards the bedroom, as she did she called behind her "Of course, unless you suffer from night terrors, you're a vampire or you snore then the deal is off!"

Jem chuckled and then paused, *'I'm a lesbian, I don't need to declare that do I? Or should I? Is it morally acceptable to get into bed with another woman without her knowing I'm attracted to women? Perhaps I could do it subtly.'* Jem snorted. *'How do you just drop that into a conversation…by the way Rachel I like boobies not pee pee's!'* Jem snorted again and shook her head in dismay before she was pulled her from her internal dilemma as Rachel's smooth timbre echoed from the bedroom.

"Are you coming Miss Shaw? I've left some PJ's on the bed for you."

With that she heard the bathroom door softly close and the running of water from the tap. Jem shook herself into action by walking into the bedroom and immediately stripped into the pyjamas, keen not to be caught semi naked as she continued to mull over her dilemma in her head. *'If I keep my distance and my eyes closed I'll be fine. I mean she's gorgeous but just because I'm gay doesn't mean I'm attracted to every woman I meet…Okay, yes she is beautiful,*

34

but hey, she could be a complete bitch and this nice girl stuff could all just be an act.'

As Jem pondered this thought she shook her head, Rachel had been nothing but thankful, polite and well-mannered and suddenly she felt guilty for the disparaging thought. Besides, if she had her Gram's seal of approval she must be genuine.

Jem unhooked her bra and pulled the soft cotton tank top over her head just as she heard the bathroom door click. As she pulled the hem over her stomach she turned to see Rachel in a long blue and white striped night shirt that curved just above her knees. The look was completed by a pair of warm looking cream fleecy socks adorned with light blue love hearts. *'How cute…argh, stop it!'* Jem's stomach fluttered just before she reminded herself again that she wasn't attracted to every woman she met and this time should be no different.

* * *

Rachel gently patted her face and mouth with the towel and replaced the toothbrush in the cup next to the sink before taking a deep breath. She couldn't remember, other than her sister and the twins, who she had last shared a bed with. It had been so long, and she had become so over-protective of her privacy, that she rarely let her guard down. She had certainly never invited a near stranger into her bed. But Jem was different, she had been so kind and thoughtful without seemingly wanting anything in return… *'yet'* her sub consciousness sneered.

Rachel threw down the towel onto the rack, disgusted with how faithless and untrusting she had become of new people. Over the last 4 years or so she had effectively cut herself off from meeting new people. *'Having a psycho stalker will do that to a girl'* she reasoned.

Everyone in the media believed she was in the middle of a divorce, but what they don't know is that Matt is a dear friend who she loves with all her heart. But marriage had simply been a convenient arrangement for them both, rather than a love match. They certainly had never consummated their marriage.

More recently Matt had realised it was time to come clean and commit to his real love, Pete. Rachel adored them both and it finally felt right for her and Matt to officially separate so that the 'process' could begin. The plan was that they would divorce, amicably of course, leave an appropriate amount of time and then he would 'come out' to the media before marrying his life partner for real.

It all looked good on paper, but in truth Rachel was scared for him. Matt, being an action star, had a lot of stereotypes to crush and it had the potential to ruin his career, as well as bringing out all of the crazies and homophobes.

On a more selfish note, she would also need to find a new cover or 'woman' up, but the thought of being back in the shark infested waters of the dating pool caused her heart to palpitate and the anxiety, she had worked hard to cover and compress, quickly reared its ugly head. *'Mark Copland, you have so much to answer for.'*

Alongside this fear of meeting new people or dealing with the inevitable 'come-ons' she also had to worry about being such an obvious public figure, in her mid-30's no less. The perfect combination in the precise equation society, and the media as a whole, used to calculate that she needed to settle down and start a family.

In reality Rachel was happy to be on her own; with no-one else to worry about, to panda to, or explain herself to, she could focus on her career and the crazy hours doing movies demanded. Simply put she really didn't have anything else to give or time to dedicate to anyone else, and that's exactly what she kept telling her chicken-shit, fear filled, self. *'I'm a coward and I know it…Any other excuses?'*

All this hard work meant that her career had skyrocketed and money was not an issue, few men could cope with being in the shadow of such a public figure, unless of course they were after the fame and money associated with her. That was the kind of relationship she wanted to avoid at all costs. They weren't based on love and even then, is it worth it? Rachel subconsciously shrugged her shoulders as she considered her own question, quietly answering herself *'I wouldn't know, I've never even been in love. Hey I'm a love virgin!'* Rather than smiling at her own joke she frowned as she exited the bathroom to find her gaze fixed on the gentle curves and flexing muscles across Jem's bare back and then her toned abdomen as she turned, simultaneously pulling down the tank top. The brushed cotton bottoms hung loosely from her slim hips, but clung to the muscles of her thighs. *'Clearly Jem is in shape, probably all that skiing.'* Rachel gave her a crooked smile as they looked at each other from opposite sides of the bed. "Which side would you like? Any preference?"

"Erm, I don't have a side so I'm not fussed. You choose." Jem's thoughts flitted briefly to Rachel's soon to be ex and her own lack of a partner. *'Rachel probably has a side, so I'm gonna have to be careful.'* Her normal routine was to lie in the middle of the bed with her limbs spread wide. In the morning her sheets were usually a scrunched mess from all of her moving about, or 'bedroom acrobatics' as her Mum used to call them when she was a kid. Thirty years of active sleeping was going to need to be restrained, she'd never had a co-habiting long-term relationship and any other bed sharing generally didn't involve much sleep!

"I'll take this side, seen as though I'm here already. I left a new toothbrush on the side for you." Rachel said as she slipped under the thick down duvet and Jem walked around the bed into the bathroom.

A few minutes later they were both snuggled under the warm quilt, Jem so close to the edge she nearly fell out as she turned on her side to look away from Rachel. Before long the room was quiet apart from the gentle rhythmic breathing of its sleeping occupants.

Chapter 4

A gust of wind howled and whistled through the wooden cabin jolting Jem awake. Momentarily disorientated she looked around the darkened room. The sloping ceiling, skylight and rough carved wooden bed were all foreign to her as she rummaged through her sleep confused thoughts to remember where she was. Then she noticed the warm delicate hand resting on the smooth skin of her stomach. *'Shit, I'm in Rachel's bed. Crap, am I on my side?'* Careful not to move and disturb her bed mate she checked her position to find that by some minor miracle she was still on her own side, so much so that another inch and one of her butt cheeks would be hanging off the bed! Rachel was snuggled into her side, her face nestled into the curve of her neck. Jem registered the warm breath across her collar bone, the swell of Rachel's breasts against her upper arm, Rachel's stomach pressed across her forearm and the hand tucked under her tank top, and that's all before acknowledging the leg thrown across her own. Jem was virtually wearing Rachel and it was making her feel hot, in more ways than one.

After taking a few moments to work out her options, Jem carefully lifted Rachel's arm by the wrist and laid it gently onto her side before shimmying sideways, dropping a foot to the floor so that she could ease the other leg free from under Rachel's thigh. With a stumble and a slip she was free before unceremoniously crumpling to the floor with a quiet "hummpphh".

Jem picked herself up and dashed to the bathroom where she flicked on the light which was stark and bright as her eyes adjusted from the darkness of the bedroom. The fan instantly began humming and she cursed quietly at the noise, hoping it wouldn't disturb the sleeping Rachel. As she cooled her flushed face and dabbed it with the towel she couldn't help thinking *'I've just been straddled by Rachel Clarke, Oscar winner and 2 time Golden Globe Award winner…straight actress in the middle of a divorce…shit.'*

On regaining her composure Jem re-entered the bedroom, bumping the bed as her eyes re-adjusted to the darkness. Rachel was still fast asleep on her side of the bed, thick blonde hair fanned out behind her, lips slightly parted as she breathed and mumbled in her sleep. Jem watched for a moment before deciding she might be getting a bit creepy and climbed into the free space on the opposite side, cuddling into the pillow. The fresh floral scent of Rachel's shampoo clung to the soft cotton sheets and before long she found herself dreaming of alternative endings to the earlier incident of Rachel's body wrapped around hers.

* * *

The dull light and quiet patter of swirling snow on the skylight gently roused Rachel from a deep sleep. With a yawn and a stretch she turned and whacked straight into Jem, who immediately opened her eyes in surprise. Just for a beat they laid with full frontal contact before they simultaneously rolled away, both rubbing their foreheads. "Sorry Jem, that was my fault I didn't realise you were there. Did I hurt you?"

"No…it's okay." Jem rubbed her head. "Did you sleep well?"

"Yeah, really well, like the land of the dead or something. I'm gonna drink schnapps before bed more often! I'm usually a terrible sleeper."

They both lay on their backs next to each other, listening to the soft pitter patter of snow on the roof.

"I wonder how deep the snow is now." Rachel pondered aloud, all the while thinking *'wasn't I on the other side of the bed?'*

"Not sure…it's early this year. I think we've got a few bad days before it clears up. Should be some good skiing though."

"Mmmm…I don't ski." Rachel said distractedly as she fiddled with her hair.

"What?! You've had this cabin here for like, what 10 years, and you don't ski. How the hell did you manage that?" Jem turned onto her side and leant on her elbow as she looked disbelievingly at Rachel.

"Well, I usually come up in the summer for one and, well, it's just too risky. I'm usually tied to a contract and stuff like skiing isn't insured." Rachel stopped fidgeting with her hair and turned to glance at Jem. "If I hurt myself I could be sued for breach of contract. It's just never seemed worth it."

"Oh? You never wanted to or has it always been work that meant you never could?" Jem asked as she repositioned herself onto her back to look up through the skylight at the ominously grey clouds above.

"I used to fancy it…watching people race down the mountain looked so exhilarating. I wondered what it would be like, but clearly not enough to actually get out there and do it."

"I'll teach you if you want? That is if you aren't tied to any contracts at the moment…I promise I'll bring you back in one piece!" Jem smiled playfully as Rachel looked over.

Rachel smoothed out the comforter with both palms before replying. "Okay, that sounds good. What can I do in return?"

"Ermmmm…what could you do in return? Hmmmm, let me think." Jem rubbed and tapped her chin with her fingers in a mock scheming pose and glanced sideways at Rachel, who simply smiled before landing the pillow across her chest. "Hey, that's not fair." Jem laughed.

"Well neither is teasing me, you deserved that." Rachel pouted

"Ahhhh, don't pout."

Rachel pouted some more. "Why?"

"Cause you look…" 'Kissable.'

"What?"

"Nothing. Errr, you could start by making me some breakfast. How about that for part one of our deal?"

"Done." Rachel leapt out of bed, groaning as she landed, clearly forgetting the bruise up her side. At a less enthusiastic and energetic pace she pulled some clothes from her drawers and made her way into the bathroom.

After breakfast the girls donned their winter gear and stepped out into the snowy air. It was agreed that they would get Rachel's groceries and stuff from the car, then Jem would head home before the next big snow storm, which was forecast to hit mid-afternoon. The forecaster had talked it up, but no amount of persuasion from Jem could get Rachel to accompany her back to town while it passed.

Jem cleared the snow off Bobby, the snow mobile, and again it spluttered and choked out a plume of blue-black smoke before Jem revved it into life. Rachel gingerly climbed onto the back and gently held onto Jem as they carefully zigzagged down the track to the abandoned SUV.

The snow twinkled like thousands of tiny diamonds as the sun peeked through the occasional break between bleak towering grey clouds that monopolised the sky.

The morning was bitingly cold and Rachel's breath clung in the air like puffs of smoke. The wind whipped against her reddening face causing her long hair, not tucked into the helmet, to flail behind her. The whole feeling was bracing but energising at the same time. For the first time in a long while she felt safe and free, without the weight of any expectation upon her. However, it wasn't long until Rachel's feeling of Zen was interrupted as they slowed to a stop.

Once they reached the edge of the hollow Jem silenced the engine and they cautiously peered over the edge of the slope to see the beat up vehicle sitting under a huge pile of snow, despite being protected by the pine tree, whose trunk it precariously leant against.

The girls looked sideways at each other and Jem nodded. "You ready?"

"Yep, let's go." Rachel replied confidently, which served more as a personal pep talk than the level of assurance she actually felt about traversing the relatively steep slope to the battered metal hulk that was her beloved truck.

They both began sliding, controlling their speed by digging their heels into the deep snow. After a few minutes they reached the car and carefully opened the back door. The car gave an ominous groan and Jem looked at Rachel. "Let's be really careful. I'll grab what I can reach. Anything else we'll have to leave. I don't want it to fall into the creek, and I certainly don't want it to take us with it."

Rachel nodded in agreement before they began working quietly and efficiently at removing the groceries and a suitcase off the back seat. The car gave another groan and the girls stepped back. Jem went to grab the last couple of bags but Rachel intercepted her arm. "Just leave it. I've got all the important stuff."

"Okay." Jem breathed, creating her own little cloud as it condensed in the bitter cold.

They began lugging the bags up the slope. It seemed to take forever, the deep snow and Rachel's injury made climbing difficult. By the time they reached the top the second time their faces were red and gleaming with sweat, despite the chilly temperature.

Most of Rachel's stuff squeezed into the saddle storage of the beat up snow mobile and Rachel pulled out the handle of the hard plastic suitcase, allowing it to be dragged behind them as they chugged up the incline back to the cabin.

All the extra weight slowed and taxed the ancient snow mobile and by the time they reached the last curve and rise in the track it coughed and came to an abrupt halt, sliding precariously backwards until the land levelled out again, slowing Bobby's momentum.

Jem swore under her breath as she tried fervently to restart the engine, only for it to throw out a potent black cloud of exhaust and wheeze like an old smoker before puttering out after a few moments. No amount of revving would coax it back into action and after a louder curse she gave up.

Jem gave Rachel a backward glance and sighed. Rachel nodded at the wordless communication and carefully dismounted the padded seat she was straddling and began wrenching the heavy suitcase up the final incline, closely followed by Jem who had both arms laden with groceries and the large carryall across her back.

By the time they reached the cabin Rachel was cursing like a sailor, her face flush with exertion and her ribs ached in protest. No doubt too breathless to talk they dumped their haul unceremoniously on the floor and plopped themselves heavily onto the sofa, still wearing their snow covered boots, thick winter jackets and salopettes.

"I'm pooped!" Rachel huffed once she'd caught her breath. Jem's low rumbling chuckle caused Rachel's lips to curve at the edges in a small smile. "What?!"

"Pooped! Is that even a word?"

"Yes…and I am. Hey and don't think I didn't notice how hard you were breathing when we got in here. I'm not that unfit."

'No you're certainly not' Jem thought.

A comfortable silence fell around them as they recovered, again watching the hypnotic flames of the fire dance and crackle. After a few moments a gentle tapping sound filtered into Jem's consciousness before it became louder and more forceful.

"Oh hell!" Jem jumped up and pressed her face against the lightly steamed up French window leading onto the veranda. The snow storm had returned and it could be seen coming in waves across the exposed hilltops above the cabin. With each second that Jem watched the storm worsened until it had become a full on 'white-out'. The seemingly soft flakes were now pelting mercilessly against the glass, as if trying to gain forceful entry into the cosy wooden cabin.

"Should we go get the snow mobile?" Rachel asked, now standing next to Jem with her arms wrapped protectively across her midriff.

"No, the snow's too heavy now." Jen said with a resigned sigh.

"But it's only 11.30, the snow wasn't meant to come 'til this afternoon."

"You try telling the snow that!" Jem frowned, a crinkle forming between her eyebrows. "I'm surprised, the forecasters are usually more accurate. They have to be for the skiers."

"Well, at least we got the groceries in. Better to have some fresh stuff rather than eating out of cans."

"Mmmm, yeah." Jem responded as she rummaged in her pocket, retrieved her phone and looked at the screen. She seemed caught up in her thoughts before suddenly springing into action. "No signal, I best see if I can radio down to Gram and let her know the change of plan. I don't want her worrying." She walked briskly over the CB radio and began calling for Lucy, using her less than complimentary call sign, but to little avail. The only thing that could be heard was muffled static interlaced with some vaguely humanlike noises. Jem relayed the message, repeating several times that she was up at the cabin in the hope that Lucy would by some miracle hear something through the static.

Once this was done there was little to do apart from settle in and get comfortable. After hanging up the snow gear Rachel wheeled the suitcase to the bedroom and Jem loaded the fire 'til it roared. The flicker of the flames and heat fought against the grey, swirling background that attacked each of the windows, warming the cosy space. The wind howled and seemed intent on forcing its way through any weaknesses in the wooden structure, making it whistle and groan. Jem stood at the window and shivered, turning as she heard the soft pad of socks on wood as Rachel returned to the lounge.

"Would you like a bath or a shower before lunch? You can go first and borrow some clothes. I don't know about you but all that heaving about in the snow left me a bit hot and sweaty."

"That would be great, if you don't mind?"

"Of course I don't. I'm just sorry that I've got you stranded up here. I should have let you go and got the stuff myself." Rachel folded her arms carefully around herself, watching out for the bruised ribs.

"No, then you'd have been stuck without any fresh groceries. Besides it isn't even meant to be snowing yet. How were we to know?"

Rachel gave a low, soft laugh that made Jem feel a little bit fluttery inside. "Yeah, I suppose."

"Right, shower it is. I can take your not so subtle hint about body odour!" Jem joked, giving Rachel a sideways look and lopsided smile as she headed for the en-suite. Just before she could open the bathroom door Rachel appeared. "Just before you go in, my clothes are in here" She pulled the top draw ajar, revealing socks and other under garments "…and the towels are in here." She snuck into the bathroom in front of Jem and grabbed a large fluffy cream towel from the chest at the end of the bath and pressed it into Jem's hand before she made a hasty retreat from the bedroom.

Jem stood and watched her leave, admiring the curves that were encased in leggings and the tight fitting long sleeved thermal top, before shaking her head and entering the bathroom fully. It was a good size and had a deep, free standing bath with claw feet at the far end opposite the door. A shower was tucked in to the left of the door and the toilet and sink to the right. Jem opted for a shower, mindful that she didn't want to use up all the hot water.

A near scalding stream of water rained down from the large round head above her, pummelling her skin, chasing away any remnants of cold. Rachel's scent surrounded her as she rinsed the suds from her hair. Jem turned off the water and leant back against the cool ceramic tiles, closing her eyes as she took several cleansing breaths and chastised herself. *'She's straight, straight, straight and getting a divorce. If anything she needs a friend, not some infatuated woman mooning over her. Get a fucking grip.'*

Jem gave a decisive nod once she had worked through her internal pep talk and got on with getting dry, only to groan in frustration when she opened the draws to find herself some fresh clothing. The top draw was filled with an assortment of underwear. *'Can I put my own underwear back on?'* She scrunched her nose at that thought. *'I could go commando...in Rachel's leggings...God no.'* With a hard swallow Jem found some underwear, exhaled loudly and then got on with finding the rest of her ensemble and dressed quickly.

As Jem entered the kitchen her senses were assaulted by the sight of Rachel efficiently dicing some vegetables and the smell and sizzle of cooking onions. She stood and watched for a moment as Rachel began humming and softly singing a tune while confidently and elegantly moving from the stove to the chopping board, clearly absorbed in her task. She had a beautiful singing voice and again Jem admired her from behind before rolling her eyes at herself in disgust.

"Can I help?"

Rachel jumped and then pressed a hand to her chest as she turned and looked at Jem. "Shit, you startled me!"

"Sorry." Jem replied genuinely. "Is there anything I can do to help?" She repeated as she stepped further into the kitchen area.

Rachel cast her gaze over the figure in front of her, sweeping over the slim frame that somehow seemed strong, but feminine at the same time.

Jem noticed and a red blush crept up her chest, into vision above the V of her t-shirt onto her neck.

Rachel quickly turned away and busied herself, popping a dish into the oven. "Nope all done, it's in the oven, should be ready in about half an hour. Do you want some fruit to keep you going?" Rachel grabbed a dish from the side and thrust it at Jem. "Here, I cut some melon into a bowl. Help yourself, I'm just going to bob into the shower." With that Rachel quickly exited the room.

'Well, that was a little awkward I hope I'm not wearing something I shouldn't?' Jem thought as she padded into the living area in her stockinged feet and folded herself onto the soft leather sofa. After a moment she reached across and grabbed something to read from the pile on the coffee table. Jem began absently flicking through a book, filled with pieces of art through the ages, but soon became more invested as she noticed the detail and skill displayed.

As she perused the images, appreciating the art, she noticed that Rachel had several oil landscape paintings hung around the room. Abandoning the book Jem casually sauntered around the room, taking time to stop and absorb the skill of the artist. Most of the oils were colourful and used bold confident brush strokes to create pieces that were on the verge of abstract, but yet it was still clear that they were portraying the natural landscape they captured.

It wasn't a hard decision to make, Jem thought they were outstanding, particularly the larger canvas that was framed above the sofa. Jem leaned forward and attempted to decipher the painter's curling signature, they were mostly by the same artist, L R Davies. She made a mental note to ask Rachel or 'Google it'. *'Perhaps I could afford a print for one of the walls at home?'*

As Jem stood at the sofa, her eyes still locked on the painting, Rachel entered looking fresh and glowing from the shower. Her long blonde hair was still wet and tied into a loose bun. She wore a pair of form fitting, well-worn stone wash jeans that revealed a hint of flesh at her knee where the material had ripped and frayed. *'Stunning'.* Jem hastily averted her gaze back to the art in front of her. "These paintings are amazing."

"Which is your favourite?" Rachel asked as she moved in front of the sofa next to Jem, brushing shoulders as they both stood immersed in the vibrant colours.

"This one, definitely." Jem pointed at the painting in front of them. "Although I do like them all, alot."

"Yeah, that's my favourite too, it's Fergal's Creek."

"Really, the creek just down the track here?" Jem asked, stretching her arm out in the vague direction of the track through the woods outside.

"Yep." Rachel nodded to confirm her words.

"Oh, you must know the artist then? I'd love to see some more of their work. I could do with some colour on my walls at home."

"Okay, I'll see what I can do." At that Rachel paused and looked back at the painting before striding across to the kitchen. After donning a large, slightly scorched oven glove, Rachel plucked the sizzling dish from the oven. "Lunch is ready."

As they consumed the meal Rachel had prepared the conversation flowed easily. They discussed a bit about art, until they realised Jem knew nothing about it and Rachel steered the conversation elsewhere. It wasn't until after they had cleared the plates and washed up that Jem realised she'd been grilled! Rachel had extracted most of her family history, favourite foods and holiday experiences, and despite chatting away for the last hour she had still only had a glimpse of the person in front of her. Rachel had talked animatedly and freely about growing up as a twin and all the mischief they had made as girls, and she clearly loved cooking, happily discussing her favourite recipes. But other than that Jem was in the dark. 'Rachel was guarded and she could understand why, living in the glare of the cameras couldn't be easy.'

As the snow continued to swirl and howl outside they occupied themselves with Monopoly, snakes and ladders, scrabble and cards. It was like they had regressed to childhood as they competed; laughing, joking and teasing each other as the afternoon eased into the evening. By 7pm they had exhausted themselves with board games and, after picking at meats and cheeses laid out on the coffee table, they sampled the cherry schnapps Rachel had bought from Lucy.

"Mmmm, homebrew, could this be lethal?" Rachel asked as she swirled the syrupy liquid in her cut glass tumbler.

"Probably, it's Mrs Alveston's. I've had some of her moonshine and it's strong enough to strip the varnish off this coffee table." Jem took a tentative sip "Mmmm, it's good; doesn't taste too strong." After sampling another sip Jem chuckled.

"What?"

"It might not taste strong but it could still be potent…Gram, Mrs Alveston and five of the other ladies in town have a Tuesday Club. They're not all old, Rita and her best friend Linda, from the restaurant, are in it too." Jem tucked her feet underneath her and turned to face Rachel on the sofa. "Well, when they first started they'd made some apple brandy. Last summer it was the 20 year anniversary of the club, so they thought they should celebrate by sampling this brandy along with some of the other food and drinks they'd tried over the years." Jem smirked and looked at Rachel, who was smiling and listening intently, clearly anticipating some drunken shenanigans as a result of this sampling. "As you can imagine they got blind drunk. Gram arrived home at midnight, in a Police patrol car!" Rachel unceremoniously dribbled as she choked down a laugh with a mouthful of homebrew. Jem smiled and continued with her storytelling. "I mean she was only down the street! She'd been picked up meandering, arm in arm with Mrs Alveston, down the middle of the highway in the wrong direction." Jem's eyes sparkled with mischief as Rachel chuckled. "And that's not the worse bit."

"No?"

Jem shook her head. "You wouldn't believe it."

"Oh, I don't know. I work with a bunch of actors who know how to let their hair down. You wouldn't believe what they can get up to…Saying that, Lucy is quite respectable I couldn't imagine her creating too much of a scene."

"You'd think." Jem adjusted her position and took another sip of the potent liquid, her deep brown eyes flashing with mirth as she continued to with her tale. "Well the only reason we knew Gram was missing was because Rita and Linda had come back to Lucy's at about 11pm and were giggling like school girls." Jem shook her head at the memory. "Rita had snapped her heal and Linda had her skirt tucked in her panties!" Rachel let out a bubbling laugh as Jem gave a lopsided grin and continued. "When Mike came to pick up Rita it became apparent that no-one knew where Gram was. Mr Alveston had rung half the town, frantic about his wife who hadn't come home yet either…Well, by this time Linda was passed out on Gram's sofa, drooling on the cushion and snoring like a 300lb man and Rita was worshipping the porcelain God, although not before she managed to throw up in my snow boots!" Jem exclaimed, crinkling her nose in disgust.

Rachel laughed again, laying her hand on Jem's forearm. "Oh no, I hope she bought you some new ones?"

Jem pouted "No, I'm still waiting."

"Oh, you poor thing!" Rachel rubbed her arm in a mock soothing gesture, her face quickly morphing from the theatrical look of understanding to a shit eating grin that revealed her true glee at hearing Jem's recounting of the mischievousness of these seemingly upstanding and respectable pillars of the community.

"And I had to clean up the puke!" Jem raised her hands in disgust, breaking the contact between the pair of them. "I tell you that is no thing you should have to do for your sister-in-law. Believe me, when that baby is a teenager they're gonna know all about their Mommy's antics! Revenge is sweet." Jem said as she rubbed her hands together in a mock scheming pose.

Rachel let out a roll of laughter that made Jem smile and set loose a single flapping butterfly into her stomach which she tried to drown with a gulp of liquor. "Anyway, back to the missing Grandmothers…I sent Mike in the truck to go look for them, while he was out the Police arrived. The officers looked well amused and when I looked in the back of the car they were both asleep in a blanket."

"Ahhh, bless."

"No! They were wearing a blanket because as they'd walked down the middle of the highway they'd stripped naked. It's a good thing it was summer or they would've got frostbite in some rather unfortunate places!"

"Oh no!" Rachel held a hand over her mouth.

"Oh yes!" Jem winked at Rachel. "We were picking up clothing for the next 2 days down that road. I'm sure the early morning commuters had a laugh when they saw Gram's bra hanging from the 'Welcome to Bradely' sign and a pair of granny pants dangling from a tree branch! Just you mention apple brandy next time you see Gram and see what she does. Honestly, those two will never live it down." Jem shook and hung her head to reiterate the words she'd spoken. "What possessed them to take off all their clothes is a mystery to me."

By now Rachel was peeling with laughter, gripping her sides. "Stop, you're making my ribs ache!" Jem simply looked over her tumbler and took another healthy gulp of schnapps as she watched strands of Rachel's hair, which had come loose from her bun, tumble around her face. Another butterfly took flight in Jem's stomach and she continued to sip the homebrew in the hope that it would still their beating wings.

The story of the drunken Grannies sparked an evening of storytelling of drunken antics and childhood pranks. Tongues getting looser as the schnapps disappeared and glasses were topped up. Rachel, always a little wary, was in charge of the bottle, topping up Jem's glass several times before she had drained it.

By 11 o'clock Rachel was a little inebriated but Jem was by far the worse for wear. Rachel hauled Jem off the couch and wrapped an arm around her middle to steady her as they walked. Jem leaned into her touch and rested her heavy, drunken head on Rachel's shoulder and sighed.

"You all right?" Rachel asked, dipping her head forward and tucking a strand of Jem's rich brown hair behind her ear so that she could see her face.

"Mmmm hmmm." Jem had her eyes closed, so Rachel held on a little tighter as she manoeuvred through the doorway and helped her onto the bed.

"Come on, let's get you into bed." Jem giggled as Rachel began pulling off her socks and reached for the hem of her t-shirt. Jem stopped laughing and seemed to snap out of her drunken daze.

"What…what are you doing?"

"I'm helping you into your PJ's. Come on, lift your arms up so we can take this t-shirt off."

"It's okay, I can do it." Jem slurred slightly, standing abruptly onto wobbly legs in front of Rachel.

"Wow, steady there tiger." Rachel reached for Jem's shoulders as her stance wavered precariously. "Maybe I should help you. Come on, it's nothing I've not seen before." She said directing her hands down her own body, which only caused Jem to focus on the areas she had just highlighted with her hands.

"Earth calling Jem!"

Jem licked her lips and raised her slightly unfocussed eyes to Rachel before shaking her head in an attempt to sober up and pull herself together, but it was no use. '*How much bloody schnapps did I drink?*' Jem thought before she felt the brush of soft hands up her sides and the t-shirt being lifted over her head. She stood mute as Rachel smirked at her.

"God, you're going have one hell of a hangover in the morning." Rachel arched an eyebrow at that sentiment before she glimpsed a line of writing up Jem's side and her eyes roamed over the milky pale skin of her toned tummy. She reached for the pyjama top and wrestled it over Jem's head. Bending down she removed the leggings, Jem resting her hands gently on top of her head as she extracted each foot from the soft clingy fabric and slipped them through the legs of the brushed cotton bottoms. As she pulled up the PJ's up she admired the toned thighs before rising to standing directly in front of Jem, who had now positioned her hands on Rachel's shoulders. Jem's eyes were black and Rachel could see the rapid beat of her pulse in her neck. '*Oh! I hadn't figured that out. Clearly Matt's gaydar hasn't rubbed off on me.*'

"All done." Rachel said gently squeezing her hands on Jem's waist, causing her to blink her eyes lazily. With a gentle push to Jem's shoulder she fell back onto the bed and Rachel pulled the comforter up over her as she curled into the foetal position, eyes already closed.

Chapter 5

Jem groaned and tried to wet her lips but her mouth was as dry as the Sahara. Her head felt heavy and a dull ache throbbed at her temples. It was still dark, so she stumbled to the bathroom to relieve herself before washing her face and downing some water, using the toothbrush cup, which made it taste a little minty.

Looking at her face in the mirror she realised she was in her PJ's. Jem took a deep breath and closed her eyes, which allowed some of the haze surrounding the previous night to clear enough to recall Rachel putting her to bed.

"Oh God!" She groaned before rubbing her palms across her face and sighing loudly.

She quickly lowered her volume when a mumble came from the bedroom. Looking around for somewhere to perch she sat on the side of the bath and removed her bra from under the soft cotton tank top she was wearing, rubbing her shoulders and sides where the straps and underwire had dug in.

The dull ache in her head was already easing so she downed another cup of water before brushing her teeth and tongue, to rid it of the remnants of last night's drinking session. Feeling refreshed she gently eased herself back into bed and quickly fell into a deep sleep.

* * *

A cold draught around her legs and the tickle of something across her face caused Rachel to wake abruptly, frantically swiping a palm over her forehead and cheek to rid it of whatever creepy crawly might have been there.

After a moment, her racing pulse calmed as she realised it was just Jem's hair. The other woman was laid diagonally across the bed, the bedcovers tangled at her feet and her head next to Rachel's, but her face was turned away. *'No wonder I'm cold!'*

With a shiver Rachel left the bed and visited the bathroom before untangling the bed cover. Standing at the foot of the bed she stifled a chuckle with a hand over her mouth. Jem's cheek was squashed into the mattress, her lips pouting and her hair a tangled mop. *'How cute!'*

Shaking her head at the situation Rachel crawled onto the bed and laid sideways, her back against the foot of the bed and her feet hanging slightly over the side in a position that matched Jem's. Pulling up the covers she dozed while the soft early morning sunlight filtered into the room and again the soft patter of snow could be heard on the sloping roof above.

Rachel must have fallen back to sleep because she awoke to the soft snuffling's of Jem, who had turned in her sleep and was facing her. Jem's features were relaxed and her eyes fluttered slightly as she dreamed. She had a smooth, slightly tan complexion and her lips were a dusky rose. Rachel allowed herself to take in the features and appreciate her attractiveness. She had the same straight nose as Lucy and her eyebrows softly curved, just like her brother Mike. She had a small hoop in the top of the exposed left ear, hinting at the rebellious streak she said she had gone through in her mid-teens.

Jem shifted slightly and a lock of hair fell across her face, blocking Rachel's view. With tentative fingers Rachel softly tucked it back behind her ear, enjoying the feel of soft, warm skin beneath her fingertips. Large brown eyes blinked open and looked directly into her own. "Hi" Rachel whispered, quickly pulling her hand back in front of herself. "How's the head?"

Jem blinked before smiling. "Fine thanks, sorry for getting sloppy drunk on you last night."

"It's okay, the Police weren't around to witness you streaking across the hilltop in the snow."

A flicker of panic crossed Jem's features before she chuckled. "Nice try. I wasn't that drunk."

"Nah, actually it's me who should be apologising to you. I was in charge of the bottle. I kept topping your drink up while you were talking."

"Aahhh, that makes sense. I thought I was just a lightweight compared to you! No wonder you were able to put me to bed…thanks for that by the way."

"You're welcome…it was very educational."

Jem's breathing faltered. "It was?"

Rachel simply nodded as Jem continued to hold her breath. "What did you learn?"

"That you have a tattoo, for one. What does it say?"

"Stay strong, love freely and be yourself kid."

"Really? Can I see?"

"Umm, okay." Jem rolled onto her back and raised the side of the soft cotton tank top, the material bunching just under her right breast.

Rachel cast her eyes down the line of neat italic writing that looked like someone had handwritten it up her side from the dip above her hip to her ribs. She delicately traced it with the tip of her finger making Jem shiver and goose bumps to raise her skin.

"Sorry."

"It's okay." Jem said as she hastily pulled the top back over her midriff.

"Can I ask, why did you…no, errr…who?"

"Its fine" Jem interrupted Rachel's rambling question and turned back on her side to face her. "My Grandad said that to me…when I came out." She added hesitantly, lowering her gaze as she fiddled with the comforter. "He died not long after and it just helped me through a tough time, you know? Kind of helped me to keep my resolve when I could have taken an easier route."

"He sounds like he had his head screwed on."

Jem jerked her head up at the unexpected response. She had anticipated Rachel to be at least mildly freaked out by her announcement, but she didn't seem bothered in the slightest.

Rachel chuckled, "You thought I was going to say something else?" Jem nodded and smiled. "So, if you don't mind me asking, what was the easier route?"

"You know, the usual." A comfortable silence stretched between them, until Jem elaborated. "Dad had some pretty strong views, and they weren't favourable towards people like me. Mom was shocked, but came around, whereas Dad could never…he could never…let's just say we haven't talked in 13 years. It was hard at first because apart from being a homophobe he was a really good Dad and we were close, but as the years have gone on it's not quite so raw." The genuine compassion in Rachel's eyes was overwhelming and Jem couldn't stand to look any more, so she rolled onto her back and looked up at the skylight. "So now you know." Hesitantly she added "I hope that doesn't change anything for you, I hoped we could be friends."

"Of course not. Christ half of Hollywood is gay!" Rachel rolled onto her back, mirroring Jem and took a deep breath, letting it out shakily. Jem turned her head and thought she spied a hint of vulnerability crossing Rachel's features before she seemed to gain some resolve and a mask of confidence slid back into place.

'*Here it comes, delayed reaction*' thought Jem.

"I'm married to a gay man." Rachel said in such a rush that it took a moment for Jem to absorb it.

Chapter 6

3 weeks later…

The ladies embraced and exchanged farewells in the brightly lit foyer of Linda's restaurant in town. The Tuesday Club had decided to welcome their newest member, Rachel, with a celebratory dinner at the local eatery. They had been so friendly that Rachel had felt a little overwhelmed with emotion at points, that is, when she could squeeze it in edgeways between conversations. *'Man, these women could talk'*, and they did, about anything and everything imaginable, plus a few things you rather they didn't…a 70 year old, 200lb woman discussing thongs was a little too much for Rachel's visual brain to handle and had resulted in her unceremoniously spitting a mouthful of wine across her plate! Fortunately only Jem seemed to notice and had proceeded to snort out a laugh that had a ripple effect of giggles around the raucous bunch.

As Rachel, Jem and Lucy stepped out onto the street an icy wind swept through, causing them to tighten their scarves and coats and link arms in a vain attempt to keep the cold at bay as they walked, huddled together, the short distance to Lucy's house which she shared with Jem during the ski season.

In the last 3 weeks since Jem had rescued Rachel they had become firm friends, something Rachel hadn't believed to be possible, given her celebrity status and the 'tell all' world of gossip that usually surrounded her in LA. There was something so honest and endearing about Jem that she felt she could confide in her without harsh judgement, and from the conversations they'd had, it was clear Jem felt the same way.

As they approached the house Rachel gently tugged her arm free from Lucy's grip. "Hey, I'm going to head straight off. Thank you for such a lovely evening, I had a great time."

"Are you sure you don't want to come in for a cup of coffee before you go?" Lucy asked as she laid her hand on Rachel's forearm.

"No. Thanks though. It's getting late and I don't want it to start snowing on my way up. I think we've got some forecast for tonight."

"Okay darlin', drive safe." Lucy leant across and gave Rachel a quick hug before making her way up the garden path which was lit with soft, warm light leaking from the large mullion windows of the double fronted house. The swirl of smoke escaping the chimney was the tell-tale sign that the stove was still alight.

Rachel gave an involuntary shiver at the cold before turning to Jem. "Okay, I'll see you tomorrow night for that bowling thing?"

"Yeah, be there or be square!" Jem joked.

"You're such a geek, you know that right?!"

"Yeah, can't help it." Rachel leaned in and gave Jem a quick squeeze.

"Drive safely please." Rachel felt Jem's hot breath against her ear as she whispered the request.

"Yes Mum!"

"That British accent keeps sneaking out, you know that right?!" Jem chuckled lightly while she shook her head at her internal monologue. *'I love your accent!'* "And don't forget to drop me a text so I know if you need rescuing…again!"

"I can drive you know, there was loads of snow! If I ever have to rescue you I'm going to milk it, just like you have, so that you know how annoying it is."

"Right, whatever!" And with one last quick hug they parted ways.

After a chilly drive on icy roads Rachel landed home, immediately firing logs onto the fire and placing the kettle on the stove. Rachel quickly typed out a 'I'm home' text with dexterous fingers before stripping out of her winter gear and pouring herself a cup of tea.

With a warm mug hugged to her chest she eyed the blank canvas on the easel, which had been placed in front of the French windows, where she would be warmed by the fire while being inspired by the landscape and weather before her. However tonight, as she sipped at the hot tea, she remained focussed on the stark white of the canvas and looked inward for her inspiration. She considered her mood and how this would look as colours, how she could portray depth and what patterns and shapes might use to communicate her current emotions. With abrupt movement she put down her cup, sloshing the tea over the edge, before launching into action, piling paint onto the mixing board and frantically mixing, before daubing colour in confident brush strokes across the white surface.

Rachel had been immersed in her painting and finally fell into bed in the early hours of the morning. Her new found enthusiasm for the canvas had resulted in a step away from her usual landscapes to more thoughtful and abstract imagery that seemed to leap from her paint brush in an unexpected way.

She found a solace in this outpouring of emotions. It freed her of some of the thoughts and feelings that, at times, weighed heavily on her mind. The new pieces were more impulsive and layered heavily with oils that stood proudly from the board.

She had produced several in the last 2 weeks, which for her was unheard of. She had sent some of these new pieces to the gallery she worked with and last week they had contacted her to say they would immediately make space for them on their walls.

Being known as a reclusive, secretive artist had its bonuses; her anonymity meant that her art had been untainted by her reputation from the acting world and she could get honest reviews by simply coming across as a collector. More importantly though, the showing and selling of her pieces had encouraged her to use the income to set up a charity that organised art workshops for kids with barriers, known as ACC or Art for Children in the Community. Again, this was all anonymous and she employed a raft of people to run the charity that had no idea who she was. Quietly observing the joy this had generated had fuelled her to show and sell more, although, if she were honest with herself this wasn't the inspiration that had led to her sudden prolific outpouring of art.

The shrill ringing of the phone startled her awake. A loud expletive crossed her lips as she looked, bleary eyed, at the alarm clock it. '*11am! Okay no need for swearing*' she internally chastised.

"Hello" she croaked out before loudly clearing her throat.

"Hello gorgeous. How are you my beautiful wife? Taken up smoking?" Matt joked with a chuckle.

"Mornin', I'm fine, just slept in!"

"Mmmm hmmm!"

"I'm in the middle of no-where, what mischief can I get up to out here?"

"Well I don't know, you tell me? You've already written off your beloved truck so I'm sure you can find yourself more bother!"

"Right." she huffed "What can I do for you this morning?"

"Well, the lawyer called earlier…" A moment of silence passed, causing Rachel to intervene.

"And?"

"I'm afraid I can no longer officially call you 'my beautiful wife'. We're officially divorced." There was a slight tone of sadness before excitement leaked through.

At a loss as to what to say Rachel asked "Do you need me to come back to LA to make some announcements then?"

"I think it would be wise. We don't want it leaking from another source. At least this way we can show a united front on this, so to speak. Make sure everyone knows it's amicable."

"Yeah, of course. Do you need me to come straight away or is tomorrow okay?"

"Tomorrow is fine babe. If you can make it here before it's too late we can all have dinner together. I'll get Pete to cook and we can write a joint statement. Does that suit you?"

"Absolutely. It's been ages, I can't wait for a good catch-up."

"Okay, text me the details and I'll arrange for Sam to come and pick you up."

"Excellent, I didn't know Sam was in town?"

"Yeah, she'll be pleased to see you. She caught that rat Steve cheating on her. She's been home a week and she's only just started looking human again. For a while there I thought she might be a full on zombie!"

"God Matt, I'm sure you're kind words have been really helpful!"

A deep chuckle echoed through the speaker. "You know what brothers are for. I'd threaten to beat him up, but she already did that!"

"Noooo!"

"Oh yes, by all accounts she copped him one in the eye before landing a swift knee in his nuts!"

"Ooooh, I bet that hurt!"

"I'm sure it did, he was naked, no layer of protection!" He chuckled with a hint of evil.

"On that note I'm going."

"Alright then, see you tomorrow night. Safe flight. Love you."

"Love you too." Rachel ended the call and flopped back under the thick downy covers to warm up and contemplate the day, before falling back to sleep.

Rachel eventually crawled out of bed after midday, booked an early flight for the next day and then busied herself with packing and getting dressed for the bowling tournament that was starting in earnest that evening. Jem had talked her into being her partner for the doubles competition and no amount of honesty about her abysmal technique and complete incompetence at the sport would deter her friend.

* * *

Jem threw herself onto the overstuffed cushions of the sofa in front of the stove, which was roaring intensely after the careful application of numerous firelighters by Lucy, who was keen to chase the cold out of the large house.

She was 'pooped'! Jem smiled as she realised that the unusual word choice of her friend had unconsciously embedded in her vocabulary. The school of 4 and 5 year olds, she had been attempting to teach how to ski, had been draining and resulted in

3 tantrums and several face plants in the snow, much to the amusement of on-lookers.

In all honesty the last thing she wanted to do was go out, but the thought of spending time with Rachel overcame her tiredness and spurred her into a hot shower.

When she finally emerged she found Lucy in the kitchen stirring a large pot of what looked and smelled like chilli.

"That smells good." She said, leaning over the pot to get a nostril full of the delicious scent.

"Mmmm, what are you all dressed up for? You scrub up well!" Lucy complimented as she reached for the seasoning and began twisting pepper into the pan from an oversized mill.

"It's the bowling tournament tonight."

"Oh, I see. Rick will be there, you all dressed up for him?!" Lucy teased.

Jem scrunched her nose in disgust. "Ugh, I hadn't thought about that."

"So, who are you all dressed up for then?"

"I'm not dressed up. Can't a girl take some pride in her appearance after being wrapped in 5 layers of thermal?"

"Of course, dear." It was Lucy's standard reaction when she thought she had it all worked out and Jem eyed her suspiciously. "So...are you meeting Rachel there or is she picking you up?"

"Uh huh, there you go." Jem threw her arms up over her head in a sign of exasperation.

"What! I was just asking. My God you are touchy tonight. I hope you're going to have something strong to drink...might help with the PMS." She added in a low mutter that didn't escape Jem's ears.

With that sentiment Jem growled, before landing a quick kiss on her Grandmother's cheek. She moved swiftly from the kitchen pulling on her thick down jacket and gloves, then stuffed a hat into her pocket. She'd spent the last 20 minutes straightening her shoulder length hair, she wasn't going to undo all that hard work with 'hat head'.

Just as she opened the door she heard the signature tune of the horn from Rachel's new pick-up truck, which she had purchased a couple weeks ago in the neighbouring town. Jem had gone with her and somehow dared her into the big black 4 x 4 that had an actual set of cow horns protruding from the bonnet above the bull bars! It was here that Jem had discovered Rachel's competitive, stubborn streak, which she had goaded and poked fun at whenever the opportunity arose.

"Bye!" Jem yelled over her shoulder as she trotted down to the awaiting beast of a vehicle.

"Howdy partner, how are you tonight darlin'?" Rachel said in a full country style American accent that belied her English heritage.

"Well hello there, I am spiffing!" Jem returned in a less convincing English accent.

Rachel simply chuckled before putting the SUV in drive and pulled out into the empty road in the direction of the bowling alley, which was on the outskirts of town. "Ready to lose at bowling?"

"I think you'll find you're teamed with me. There is no way we are losing Rachel." Jem said in a serious tone.

"You say that, but you've never seen me throw a ball let alone a bowling ball!"

"We'll be fine." Jem said and then sat quietly for a moment.

Rachel glanced across at her friend, who had gone quiet and was pensively gnawing on her lip. "What's up?"

"Ugh, Rick is going to be there." Her arms rose at her sides in frustration.

"And? I thought you told him." Rachel said as she kept her eyes on the road in front of her.

"Yeah he knows, but it hasn't deterred him." She was quiet for a moment before adding, "If he's too much can we just go? Please, I can't be doing with the scene he always creates and I'm fed up of 'coming out' to him every time I see him. He just won't take 'no' for an answer." Her voice had turned from a whine into a weary lilt.

Upon sensing Jem's mood she responded in a way which she hoped would make her break into a smile. "Well you are one fine looking woman!" Rachel slipped back into her American country accent again and finished with a click of her tongue and a theatrical wink, but seeing the pout on Jem's face she sighed loudly before adding "…Fine, whatever makes you happy. But you should also know that I'm not going to be around for the next week or so. You'd better make the most of me while you can!"

"Oh?"

"Matt phoned this morning to let me know that the divorce has come through and I need to go and make the appropriate announcements." It was Rachel's turn to sound weary now.

"You okay with that?"

Rachel pulled into a parking space and looked at the concern marring Jem's beautiful features. "Yes, it's what we wanted. I just know that there is going to be some kind of media frenzy over this and I was enjoying the quiet. It could get a little mad for a while again."

A moment of silence passed, Jem nervously rubbed her palms up and down her black denim clad thighs, before voicing her main concern. "Are you coming back?"

Rachel turned to face her friend fully and captured her hands in her own. "Yes, of course I am. This is my home…in all truth I've pretty much decided to take a year off, at least from making movies and just, you know, be."

Jem nodded, reassured by the contact and Rachel's sincere words. "Okay, but if you need anything you know where I am, right?" Jem gave Rachel's hands a squeeze before pulling hers free.

"I'll be fine. It just becomes a bit of a covert mission to get back here without being followed, so it might be a couple of weeks before I land back. Plus, it gives me chance to go and see Sarah, Jack and the twins."

"That'll be fun, I bet they miss you?" Jem said as they began exiting the truck.

"What?" Rachel asked as strode to catch up and linked arms with Jem as they made their way across the snowy car park.

"I said 'I bet they miss you'."

"Yeah…and I love teasing Jack. It's like the on-going practical joke."

"What do you mean?" Jem asked as she reached for the front door to the bowling alley, effectively releasing herself from Rachel's arm.

"Well, Sarah and I, we're identical in virtually every way, apart from our personalities…but that's easy to imitate."

"That is so mean!" Jem snickered as they swapped their shoes for bowling shoes.

"I know, once we got him so good that after I left he wouldn't touch Sarah for 3 days until he was convinced it was her!"

"Oh my God, what did you do?!"

"Oh nothing, don't forget he's my sister's husband! But he gets paranoid and we play on that. We usually swap clothes and I pretend to be her and vice versa."

Jem smiled and shook her head as they made their way along the wooden path, the bowling shoes making a soft slapping noise as they walked. To their left were a line of booths filled with people chattering and drinking, most donned bowling shirts with team names emblazoned on the back and front. To their right were several bowling lanes. A few were empty, but the others had some very serious looking competitors who were lobbing the balls down the pale wooden corridors at some hellish speeds, scattering the pins loudly.

As they moved further into the retro looking space, whose walls were adorned with neon lights, battered old metal signs and quirky objects, like the grills from old cars and bikes, amongst other things, they eventually found an empty, semi-circular booth with a red velvet bench and curved wooden table, that matched the pale wood of the bowling lanes.

Both women heaved off their jackets before settling into the booth and ordering drinks and snacks on the small touch-screen tablet at one end of the table.

"Okay, you ready to have a go?" Jem asked as she began sliding out of the booth.

71

Rachel watched Jem's progress before realising she was waiting for her to join her at the lane directly opposite their booth. "Let's do it. But I'm warning you, it's been 10 years since I've done this and I was pretty crap back then too!"

Jem launched into full teacher mode, adjusting Rachel's grip, stride and throw. By the time the competition was due to start Rachel had even managed to knock over some pins and not just loose her ball down the gulley at either side of the lane!

Once the competition had begun it was clear there were 2 types of competitor; those down for a laugh and a bit of fun and those who were in it to win it and took the game very seriously. Once a full rotation of the pairs had been completed the top 2 entered a knock-out. Out of the 6 teams competing Jem and Rachel had come in 4th, which Rachel was pretty impressed with, considering that no matter how much last minute coaching Jem had given her, she was still totally useless!

The evening had flown by and now that they were officially out of the competition they relaxed in their booth chatting, drinking soda. The evening was going swimmingly until Rick appeared at the end of their table.

"Hey there ladies. I've been watching you play, that's some good butt action you've got going there Jem."

Rachel rolled her eyes, what the hell kind of come-on was that?! It was true, Jem did have a good throwing posture, but no-one with any manners would say it like that out loud.

"Hi Rick." Jem said with a sneer.

"Well, aren't you going to offer me a drink? You look fine in that tight t-shirt."

Rachel rolled her eyes again and finding Rick's arrogance hard to believe she couldn't resist. "Actually Dick, she's with me tonight."

Rick raised his eyebrows and, for what seemed like the first time, looked at Rachel. "Well now, maybe that's all the more reason for me to join you gals. Put a bit of meat in that sandwich."

"Ugh, Rick, you are such a letch." Jem retorted.

"Well, I know I can't let the ladies down, you wouldn't know what to do without a man like me!"

Rachel took in the muscles flexing on his arms as he leant forward over the table in a domineering stance. He had a strong stubbled jaw and from the open V-neck of his bowling shirt, a clump of sandy coloured chest hair was protruding. He was kind of ruggedly handsome, but his attitude and demeanour disgusted her and he'd inadvertently thrown down a challenge she was more than happy to win.

"Really!" Rachel sneered at Rick before leaning across to take Jem's face in her hands, laying her best Hollywood screen snog upon her full, dusky pink lips.

* * *

Through-out the evening Jem had to reign in her emotion. Rachel was so 'touchy feely', forever taking her hand or touching her arm during a conversation. Adjusting her bowling stance had taken virtually all of her will power, which had left her feeling conflicted. She had the best friendship with Rachel. They got on so well, conversation came freely and easily without any effort and Jem felt she could talk to her without worry of reproach or judgement. On top of that she had a great sense of humour that could lighten Jem's mood instantly. When combined with her slender body, an ease of movement and pure sensually, that Jem was sure she didn't even realise she exuded, Rachel had Jem tied in

73

knots. Jem knew she was falling for her friend, despite her best efforts to resist.

Jem was silently pondering these thoughts as Rachel was relaying a disastrous outtake involving a small boy with a line of snot that was level with his knees. Rachel flailed her hands and went from fits of giggles to gagging as she described the snot that was swinging precariously, until the child would sniff it back up his nose, only to release it again with the next act of his tantrum. Rachel was glowing and Jem was laughing soundly, while her internal monologue faltered from chastisement at her obvious adoration to simply being in awe of the beautiful person in front of her.

The story was rudely interrupted as a shadow fell across the table and the bulk of Rick leaned over to invade their space. Jem despised Rick and his sexist, homophobic attitude and pathetic attempts to hit on her. She was about at the end of her tether when she heard a stern "Right" from Rachel who had a steely, determined look in her eyes.

Before she could react Rachel had leaned over, grasped her face and firmly placed her lips over her own. The kiss was firm, yet soft. Jem felt her heart rate increase with anticipation, but she held back, allowing Rachel to lead the kiss she had unexpectedly initiated. But Rachel never deepened the kiss and no passion seeped into it. In a matter of seconds it was clear this was for 'show'.

Finally, after 20 seconds or so, Rachel pulled away and then gently pecked another kiss onto the startled Jem's lips and released her face. Rick was stood at the end of the table, open mouthed. Jem registered the look of achievement on Rachel's face and Rick's surprised expression before a flush of embarrassment and annoyance spread over her.

"Right." Rick swallowed before straightening and hastily making his escape.

Rachel smiled and nodded her head. "That showed him."

Jem looked at the retreating back of Rick and the smug look on Rachel's face. She bowed and shook her head in dismay as she had remembered how, for a few fleeting moments, she had anticipated the life altering kiss, then realised *'she's straight and an actress…a famous actress…what the fuck.'*

Embarrassed at her own delusion and clear desire, plus the humiliation of Rick and the public display of affection, Jem felt the heat rise into her cheeks and unwanted tears to fill her eyes.

Turning and blinking to hide the emotion, she rose from the booth, grabbed her coat and hastily exited the busy bowling alley. Walking at a fast clip, she pulled on her coat, gloves and hat and turned onto the road back into town. She heard Rachel call her name, but Jem simply bowed her head and walked with determination, ignoring the plea from her friend. *'From my friend…geez, I need some space or I'm going to royally fuck this up.'*

* * *

Rachel looked in astonishment as Jem grabbed her coat, back turned to her, and swiftly left the bowling alley. *'What the fuck? Have I just messed this up? Shit.'* Rachel sat planted in her seat while the realisation washed over her. She bowed her head and tears filled her eyes. *'Crap. The last thing I would ever want to do is hurt Jem.'*

Sucking in a deep breath, Rachel steadied her emotions and put on the mask she had mastered over the years to cover the turmoil inside. She grabbed her coat, pulling it on swiftly as she followed the trail blazed by her friend a few moments ago. *'Gees, my 'friend'. What was I thinking? All she wanted was to do was avoid a scene with Rick…In fact, she always pulls away from my touch, what the hell was I doing kissing her?'* Rachel's thoughts raced as she exited the bowling alley.

"Jem…Jem!" Rachel could hear the emotion in her voice as she called out to the retreating woman's back. But Jem kept on walking, bowing her head slightly.

"Oh fuck!" Rachel slammed her fists down onto her thighs. She looked around the empty car park and let a sob escape her. *'I just fucked up the one right thing in my life right now. Why can't I fucking do anything right?'*

Rachel jumped into 'The Beast' as Jem had affectionately called it, *'argh'*, and roughly started the engine, revving it harshly into life. She slammed it into drive before taking a deep breath, shaking her head, and calmly putting it back into park. After a moment of consideration she slammed her palms against the steering wheel. *'Being angry and emotional behind the wheel was going to serve no purpose for anything or anyone.'* Taking another soothing breathe she twisted the key again, silencing the engine and sat looking out into the dark night. Jem had disappeared from view.

Glancing quickly at her watch she could see it was 11pm. It was too late to phone Sarah or Mum, but Matt and Pete would still be up. She pressed the speed dial and a deep voice greeted her.

"Hey gorgeous wife of mine."

"Hey, ugly spud of a husband, we need new tag lines." Her tone was flat and Matt knew immediately that something was amiss.

"You want to talk to me or that handsome man of mine?"

"Yeah." A sob escaped past the lump and she swallowed it down as best she could, but she knew it was out there. Pete's soothing voice came over the line. "Oh babe, what's a matter? I hate it when you're sad."

"I've fucked up." Rachel whispered.

"Hey, it happens to the best of us…Take a moment…deep breath…better?" After no response he continued. "I love you…mistakes happen." Again nothing. "Rachel, what's happened? You want to talk it through?"

Rachel released a weary sigh and sniffled. After a moment she finally found her voice. "No, yes, no. Oh God I think I just royally fucked it up with Jem."

"What happened?"

Rachel quickly summarised the events, plus the kiss. Pete listened before responding. "Mmmm, maybe you need to put yourself in Jem's shoes, ya know? Hey, it was a mistake, if you are truly friends you'll be able to work it out."

Rachel sighed loudly down the handset. "Yeah, you're right, I hope. Thanks"

"You're welcome. You know I love you and I'll be here…we'll see you tomorrow, right?"

"Right…tomorrow." Rachel sniffled again before finding some strength. "I'll see Sam at the airport at 3pm, yeah?"

"Absolutely. Looking forward to seeing you. Love you gorgeous."

"Love your ugly mug too…Bye"

Rachel swiped the tears from her face, straightened and twisted the key in the ignition. The beast roared into life and she carefully pulled out of the car park onto the desolate road. After a few minutes she spotted Jem in the distance, who was still walking at speed. She was nearly in town and probably only 10 minutes from Lucy's house. Rachel pulled into the layby just in front of Jem and got out of the truck on slightly wobbly legs. As Jem approached her she slowed her pace and then stopped, leaving a healthy distance between them. Rachel spoke first.

"I'm sorry, I've clearly fucked up…The last thing I would ever want to do is hurt you…So, I'm going to apologise, then get back into the truck and go." Rachel looked down at her hands, before glancing back up to look Jem in the face. "I don't want to fuck up any more so I'm just going to give us both some space…But, I just want you to know that you've become one of my closest friends and I hope you can give me another chance?" Rachel wrung her hands together as Jem stood rooted to the spot, her arms clasped protectively around her middle. "…Okay, I'm going to…I'm gonna go now and I'll hopefully see you next week."

Rachel turned and began climbing back into the truck when she heard a quiet "Okay" from Jem. Turning her head she saw Jem give a subtle nod of agreement. Rachel resisted the urge to run over and hug the forlorn looking figure, who was stood sadly at the roadside, until she was forgiven, instead she bowed her head, climbed into the oversized black truck, started the engine and slowly pulled out of the layby.

In her rear view mirror she saw Jem resume her walking, her shoulders held stiff and head bowed low. As she approached Lucy's house Rachel drew the vehicle to a stop and waited, with the engine running, until she saw Jem turn into the drive way. Satisfied that Jem had made it safely home she made her way back to the cabin.

Once Rachel had successfully navigated the track and turned off the engine her emotional turmoil and anger at herself resumed. First she slammed the door of the truck, then the house door before yanking off her coat, which got caught in her long wavy blond hair, causing a deluge of angry expletives to tumble from her lips as she tugged and pulled fruitlessly in frustration. After screaming out her anger Rachel took a deep breath, calmed her jerky movements and, with shaky hands, simply unhooked the trapped hair. With an eerie calm she placed her jacket carefully on the hook on the side of the hearth.

By the time she had walked across the room to put a canvas onto the easel the anger had given way to regret and sadness which caused tears to flow unceremoniously down her cheeks, dropping off her chin onto the honey coloured hardwood floor. Rachel swiped roughly at her face and envisaged the canvass as she filled a tumbler with the potent cherry brandy, triggering a fresh wave of tears as she remembered the night she had first sampled the homebrew with Jem.

Setting the tumbler of brandy on the side she pulled out her paints and began furiously mixing. As the paints collided and blended on the palette her emotions settled and she found a strange feeling of tranquillity settle over her. Looking at the empty board in front of her, she pictured Jem…not her appearance, but how she made her feel and the personality that had coloured her life for the past 4 weeks. As she swept the brush and scraped the loaded the palette knife across the canvas she felt an unexpected emotion. Love, not the kind between friends, but something deeper, something she had never experienced before.

The realisation caused the emotional dam to burst again and the tears resumed their silent path over her cheeks, dripping down her chin into the paints.

'How could I let this happen? She's my friend.'

'Even if anything could happen, who in their right mind would want any involvement in the crazy world of a celebrity?'

79

'Let's face it, even though we've shared, she still barely knows anything about my bat-shit crazy life…fucking stalkers…life on film sets…anonymous art work…gees, why is my life so complicated?'

'What a mess! I'm a mess!'

As her thoughts collided between her desires and harsh reality she continued the fluent strokes across the canvas, transforming it from nothingness into the most emotive piece she had ever painted.

Chapter 7

Rachel pulled the baseball cap low over the brunette wig with one hand and tugged the small silver suitcase behind her. The baggy wide boy jeans were slung low on her hips and trailed on the floor, getting caught under the red converse sneakers. To any onlooker who glanced her way she looked like a mildly unkempt student.

Rachel kept her head bowed low and rolled her shoulders forward to give a slightly awkward teenage stance. The news had hit the headlines that morning and Matt had text and phoned to warn her about the media frenzy that had ensued.

After making it through the busy airport foyer she met Sam parked near the entrance in an old, banged up red car. On spotting each other they embraced for a long time, Rachel's suitcase sticking out behind her, tripping any unobservant passers-by. Sam sobbed into Rachel's shoulder and she held her sister-in-law tightly in a one armed embrace.

Sam sniffed heavily and roughly swiped the tears from her face. "Hey, I missed you."

"Hey baby, I missed you too…men stink!" Rachel soothed gently into Sam's ear.

A small chuckle escaped Sam as she finally released her and unlocked the car. Rachel shoved the small suitcase into the compact boot space of the well-loved red Peugeot 205. As she slumped into the passenger seat she let a long sigh escape her, before lovingly rubbing her hand across the side of the seat and then the dashboard.

"You brought her, I can't believe she's still going. It feels like forever since I shipped her over from England."

"Yeah, she looks a little beat up, but her engine has been well looked after." Sam gave Rachel a watery smile before starting her up and pulling out into the busy, slow moving traffic.

Rachel looked across at the younger woman, her long brown hair was shoved in a messy ponytail which poked out the back of a New York Yankees baseball cap, her clear blue eyes were red rimmed and slightly puffy from the earlier spill of emotion. If Sam hadn't been so caught up in her own issues she would have spotted the same, if not well concealed, symptoms in the actress sat beside her. As it was Rachel was keen to divert attention and enjoy the company of the younger woman whom she loved as dearly as if she was her own baby sister.

"So, tell me what happened."

Sam launched into the tale of 'Steve the Rat' as they edged through the traffic and then around the camp of media that was blocking their driveway. Fortunately when they had renovated they had included a well concealed back entrance that had totally proven to be worth all the hassle it had taken to construct.

On entering the house Rachel was swept from one bear hug to another as first Matt then Pete welcomed her home. After the initial contact Pete held her at arm's length and gave her head to toe assessment before hauling her into another long embrace, whispering quietly into her ear. Rachel listened, nodding and then eventually crooned quietly into the side of Pete's neck as his kind words and quiet understanding reached straight to the heart of the issue. When Rachel finally came up for air Matt and Sam had left the kitchen, leaving her and Pete to compose themselves.

Pete looked at her with a look of love and compassion as she swiped at her tears and tugged at the neck of his soggy t-shirt. "Sorry, I seem to have got you a bit damp!"

"I love you too sweetheart."

"How did you know?"

He shrugged his broad shoulders and a small smile curved his full lips. Pete was a handsome guy, and like Matt was a 6 ft 2" model of muscly male perfection. "Who wouldn't find me and Matt attractive?" He joked. "And yet you…you just loved us…no jealousy, no animosity…no ulterior motive…just sincere love and affection. You've not been happy for a while and it's not just been this stalker stuff, right? I could've been wrong, but some stuff just seemed to bring back memories of my life 10 years ago. I'm a firm believer that you fall in love with the person, not the gender. Am I right?"

"It would appear so." Taking a deep breathe she swiped a finger under her eyes and drew herself up to her full height. "Okay, that's it. No more self-pity. Let's get this divorce announced and get the ball rolling on converting you from an illicit affair into a loving husband!"

* * *

The week passed by in a swirl of announcements to the media camped out in front of the house and then onto several talk shows. Matt, Pete and Rachel decided it was time to come clean, more or less anyway, with no more hiding.

The celebrity gossip pages were set alight and no amount of honesty would quell their belief that they had been having some scandalous threesome or that Matt was Rachel's beard too, which they denied fervently. It all seemed kind of ironic following her 'eureka' moment before she left Bradely, but she did what she had been instructed by her publicist.

'Anyway, a few well-placed dates with some male eye candy would soon quash the rumours, if I want? Perhaps next time I'm back in LA Sandy could set something up?'

Nevertheless the truth was out on their side, Matt and Pete could marry. If Matt's career took a hit they could cope with that. Pete and Matt had carefully invested and set up savings accounts when they realised this was what they wanted for the long-term. Rachel had already allocated a 'time-out', which she was desperate to resume by the time she had experienced several days of Hollywood insanity and, she knew, acting wasn't the only string to her bow.

After several days of to-ing and fro-ing and showing a 'united front' the main spotlight was on Matt and Pete, so Rachel took her opportunity to make an escape. Although it was fantastic to see Matt, Pete, Sam and of course their publicist Sandy, it had been too frantic to catch-up with anyone else and Rachel was looking forward to returning to her true home in the northern hills. *'Hopefully away from the chaos and gossip.'*

Although the media had been keeping a careful eye on their Hollywood mansion, Rachel managed to sneak out in the back of a laundry van, driven by Sam. Having being stalked in a scary way 4 years ago, she had become very wary, and began a series of flights to reach her sister and Mum, who were based in Washington State.

Being a twin helped too and, as she visited, she and Sarah were careful never to be spotted at the same time. Her trip coincided with Thanksgiving which, being a holiday that wasn't celebrated in England, meant that it was relatively new for them. But they indulged heartily and, since they had arrived in America, allowed themselves to be swept up in the excitement.

All in all it had been 3 weeks of chaos and love from those who she cared for the most in the world. The only person she had truly missed was Jem. They had shared a few light-hearted texts, which helped settle her nervousness a little, but either way she was anxious to be home and fix the mess she had caused at the bowling alley.

* * *

Jem had tossed and turned all night, embarrassed and infuriated at her reaction to the events that had unfolded at the bowling alley. Having started her period in the early hours, most of her inexplicable anger at Rachel had dissipated, leaving a hollow feeling of dread in its place. But pride held her firmly in bed, going to Rachel before she left for LA to explain the whole chain reaction of emotions and reveal her true feelings would be too mortifying. As well, Rachel would no doubt have rebuffed them in the most considerate of ways, because, let's face it, she was one of the kindest and most considerate people she had ever met. The thought made her burrow down deeper under the duvet where she eventually fell into a listless sleep.

After stewing in her room for the entire day and night Jem finally peeled herself out of her pyjamas and into thermals, ready to lead the onslaught of children and adults who needed to be taught how to ski. It only took her 10 minutes to remember that, on the whole, she loved her winter job. Therefore she threw herself back onto the slopes with a new found vigour.

If she wasn't teaching she was racing down the black runs and testing the off-piste powder. By filling her down-time with adrenaline pumping runs she found that she had little time to think and by the evening she was so shattered that she would fall immediately to sleep, only to have her dreams filled with vivid images, replays and fantasies of the woman she was trying so desperately to banish to the 'friends zone'.

Her resolve to have zero contact while Rachel was away deteriorated, and after five days she dropped her a text:

Jem: 'An illicit threesome! I would never have guessed!'

Rachel: 'Well you know me, wild to the core!'

Jem: 'I think Mrs Alveston beats us both. She demonstrated how to pole dance at Tuesday club this week!'

Rachel: 'Wow, not sure if I'm glad or disappointed I missed that!'

Jem: 'Glad, definitely glad. She had gold hot pants on under her skirt to complete the ensemble!'

Rachel: 'Bloody hell! How are your eyes?'

Jem: 'My life is ruined! I'll never see a woman in hot pants the same again!'

Rachel: 'Shame, in my last movie I wore a pair of red ones! ;)'

'Well, how do I respond to that? Is she flirting? No surely not. Either way, I'm gonna have to rent that movie…to punish myself further! Get a grip, she's straight.'

Jem: 'Was there a pole?'

Rachel: 'No'

Jem: 'Mrs Alveston wins then!'

Rachel: 'I'll tell her that next time I see her. She might be tempted to give you a private showing'

Jem: 'NOOOOOOOO!!!!!'

The playful banter lifted Jem's mood considerably and then in the second week of Rachel's absence things only got better.

On Tuesday the chief of local paramedic station, James Roly, had been in contact and offered her a job. She had tried and failed to get a job at Kolton, the next town over, for years. They were referred to, rather morbidly, as 'dead men's shoes' and rarely came up. Jem had accepted immediately and was due to start her new position in the New Year. The only drawback was that she would have to cut her ski tuition short, but it was an opportunity not to be missed.

Lucy, Mike and Rita had been ecstatic and promptly took her out for a celebratory dinner at Linda's. Rita, Mike's wife who was 7 months pregnant and looked like she had swallowed a soccer ball, seemed the most relieved. Her folks lived 4 hours away and knowing Jem was on her doorstep seemed to lift a weight off her labour anxious shoulders.

"You only want me for my paramedic skills." Jem joked once the dinner plates had been cleared and they relaxed into their seats, sated and sleepy from the vast quantities of food they had consumed.

"You betcha!" Rita winked back her reply as she rhythmically rubbed her palm across her bulging stomach.

"Well, if I do deliver your first born then he or she will have to be named after me."

"That's fine Puddle Duck, whatever you say! Anyone for pudding?" They all groaned as Rita reached for the desert menu.

Once they'd had their fill and bid each other farewell, Mike and Rita waddled in one direction and Lucy and Jem in the other. Lucy had a tight grip on Jem's arm as they stepped carefully across the sidewalk, which had recently been frosted with a fine layer of snow. Their breath transformed into small puffs of cloud, which whirled around them as they walked through the freezing air.

"You know you can live with me Jem? I love having you around…" Jem squeezed Lucy's arm and turned to interrupt when Lucy continued. "No interrupting. What was I was saying…oh right, I don't want you to feel like you have to live with me."

"But I love living with you Gram." Jem successfully interjected.

"Right now you do, but what about when you find yourself a girlfriend, or have your friends over? Hmmm? So, the flat over the shop is empty. I know it needs some work, but if you're interested it's yours."

Jem stopped walking. "Really?"

"Absolutely."

Jem embraced the older woman in a tight hug. "Thank you, I would love that."

"You're welcome."

The very next morning Jem started in earnest, cancelling the lease on her old flat, calling her old paramedic station to let them know she wouldn't be re-applying and, finally, walking around her new apartment.

She had no ski lessons timetabled until that afternoon and was determined to clear out the old lino flooring and dog eared carpet. The flat only had one bedroom, but the living room was a good size with a galley kitchen off to one side. The bathroom was surprisingly large with an old roll top bath that with some refurbishment would look stunning. Unfortunately everything else would need to be replaced, but she had enough saved for the local handyman to sort this.

By the time she was on the slopes teaching that afternoon she had bought some paint and supplies, booked the moving van and handyman, who was surprisingly available, and lifted the old carpet. Jem had a renewed zing in her step and was determined that she would paint the living room when she finished this evening.

After a whirlwind of a week Jem had pushed herself to breaking point. Even though there was no rush she had moved her stuff the 60 miles from her old apartment. John, the handyman, had retiled and plumbed in the new suite into the bathroom, leaving the roll top bath of course, and had helped her to sand and then varnish the wooden floorboards. Lucy and the older ladies from the Tuesday club had run her up some curtains and now, in the early hours of Monday morning, she was sat on her beloved battered brown leather sofa, feet up on the oak coffee table in *her* cosy living room.

The old stove looked brand new with its fresh lick of black, which was at sharp contrast to the bright red embers that crackled and danced behind the newly polished glass front. The room was softly lit by scented candles that were fighting a losing battle against the smell of new paint. Jem gave a satisfied smile and her eyes drooped as she fought, unsuccessfully, against sleep.

When she awoke, cold and with a crick in her neck, she found she still had a tumbler of cherry brandy clung to her chest. As she looked at the burgundy liquid she gave a sad smile at the bittersweet memories it elicited.

Rousing herself from the saddening direction of her thoughts, Jem heaved her aching body from the sofa and into bed, vowing that tomorrow she would try out the roll top.

Chapter 8

As Rachel stepped out of the dingy elevator, onto the third level of the secure airport car park, she spotted 'The Beast'. Its horns reflected the fluorescent overhead lights, catching her eye as she made her way wearily over to the large pick-up. The flash of the indicators and 'pip' of the alarm being de-activated echoed eerily off the concrete walls, sending an involuntary shiver up Rachel's spine. She picked up the pace, slamming the lock on the door the moment her bum hit the cold, black leather of the seat.

Rachel was bone-achingly tired from the 'cat and mouse' escape from the media, who had eventually found their way to Sarah's house. She knew she needed to get back to the cabin.

The cold seat, combined with the roar of the engine jostled the actress into life as she embarked on the hour long journey home through the inky blackness, broken only by the white pin-pricks of stars that, as she drove away from the city, shone more brightly until the constellations could be clearly seen, transforming the unyielding dark into a mesmerising show that reminded Rachel of how insignificant she really was.

The clear night meant that the temperature had plummeted to well below freezing. Rachel hadn't called Lucy, so the cabin was dark and cold as she entered. Rachel didn't mess about, after throwing the deadbolt on the door she strode purposely across the living room and turned up the thermostat and clicked on a few lights.

The intensity of the media, being followed and barraged by questions and cameras, had brought the reality of being a celebrity back into the forefront of her mind, and along with it, the painful memories and fears of being stalked.

'Jem would never want any of that. That's even if she even wanted me in the first place…and let's face it, for the last week or so I've spent most

of the time denying I'm gay! I've not exactly communicated my
availability, more like pushed her away. Crap, I'm so conflicted.'

Everything at the cabin was as she left it and for the first time in 3 weeks she felt herself relax. Too tired to do anything else she stripped out of her clothes, found a pair of warm pyjamas and fleecy socks then settled into the comfy queen sized bed. The thick down duvet swaddled around her in a safe, warm cocoon lulled her into the most settled sleep she'd had since she'd been away.

'Bloody hell, it's good to be home.'

* * *

Rachel's breath caught in her throat as she grappled with her assailant. Her legs were bound together and no amount of flailing would release her. As she struggled she could feel the panic rising and the heat blaze on her skin. The fear of being trapped jolted her awake, her hair a wild mess across her face, sweaty from her struggle against the duvet, which was tightly wrapped around her legs.

Untangling herself and heaving herself up against the headboard she realised the whole cabin was like a sauna. Sunlight streamed in through the Velux window and, as she peered up, she could only detect the faintest of wispy clouds held aloft in the pale blue sky.

"Right lazy bones, it's a sign. Get out of bed and get a life!" Rachel declared to herself loudly, shaking off the residual fear from her nightmare as she flung herself unceremoniously out of the bed and quickly padded down the hall to turn down the thermostat. As she made her way back to her room she peeled herself out of her sweat drenched pyjamas, streaking down the empty corridor and into the bathroom, only to emerge a few moments later to grab her phone and quickly type out a message to Jem, who she was keen to make amends with.

Rachel: 'Hi, just to let you know I'm back in town. Hope we can catch-up soon, let me know when is good for you. Rx'

She re-read it twice. *'That's the right level for friendly, right? Shit, second guessing a simple text message is not a good sign!'* And with that she pressed send and flounced, butt naked, back into the bathroom for the long, hot shower she had been craving since she got off the plane last night, but was too knackered to take.

Half an hour later she emerged in a puff of steam, still only wearing her birthday suit in the cabin that still resembled a Swedish sauna. Her phone registered a message, received not long after sending it.

Jem: 'Up the mountain. Will ski to you.'

As Rachel set down her phone she heard a knock at the door which startled her. *Shit!* She ran to the bedroom door, only to run back for her dressing gown which was hanging on a hook on the back of the bathroom door. As she jogged down the corridor she yanked it over her shoulders and pulled the cord tightly around her waist. As she opened the front door she found Jem knocking the snow off her hat.

"Hey stranger, what have you been doing? You look like you've been through a snowdrift!"

"Hey!" Jem stepped over the threshold and pulled Rachel into a tight embrace. "Good to see you." She responded, her voice muffled, as she glanced a kiss across Rachel's cheek.

Rachel shuddered as Jem's cool lips and hot breath triggered an attack of goose bumps across her skin, but other than the obvious physical reaction, Rachel could feel herself immediately relax at Jem's friendly welcome. The weight of worry that had sat in heavily on her shoulders and in the pit of her stomach, floated way with the simple greeting. *'Perhaps the distance has been good for us both.'*

Despite Rachel's wondering thoughts, what she actually said was "Oooh, you're cold. Come in."

Rachel stepped back, checking her dressing gown was still secured as she invited Jem into the warm cabin. She hastily folded her arms loosely over her chest, mainly to hide the puckering nipples that were standing proudly through the thin material of the robe.

"Sorry!" Jem chuckled as she cast her eye properly over the woman in front of her. "You do know it's like, what, 12 o'clock?!"

"Running away from the media wore me out." Rachel threw over her shoulder as she led Jem into the kitchen, her bare feet slapping quietly on the warm wooden floorboards. "Cup of coffee?"

"Please." Jem wrenched her ski boots off, then unzipped and removed the warm thermal jacket to reveal a closely fitting, long sleeve, thermal t-shirt tucked into the low slung hipster waist of her salopettes.

As Rachel turned, two steaming mugs in her hand, she froze, her gaze travelling over the lean, yet curvy frame of Jem's torso. When Jem looked up from fixing her hair she caught Rachel staring. "You okay?"

After shaking her head slightly, Rachel smiled brightly at Jem and handed her a mug. "It's just really good to see you." *'Get a grip Clarke'* she chastised. *'Remember, crazy celebrity life not for gorgeous, lovely, caring, honest, gorgeous…already said that…Jem.'*

"It's good to see you too." Jem paused and then took a deep breath before adding. "Look, I'm really sorry for being an *arse* when you left. There was no need for it. I'm sorry."

Rachel raised an eyebrow. "Arse?!"

Jem just smiled sadly and gave a slight nod.

Rachel bowed her head, nodded lightly and began fiddling with the sash around her waist. "No, it's me who should be apologising. I made a scene, took a liberty and…" She sighed heavily and looked directly into the soft brown eyes across from her. "I fucked up. I'm so sorry I upset you, that was the last thing I wanted."

"Yeah, I don't think it was the shiniest moment of our friendship, for either of us."

"Perhaps not." Rachel looked into her coffee before again turning her gaze back onto Jem and holding her in place with honest blue eyes. "But it taught me *a lot*…I don't want to lose our friendship. It made me realise how important it is to me…and thinking that you might not forgive me really hit home in an unexpected way."

Jem explored Rachel's face. "What do you mean?"

Rachel shifted her weight and tugged at her dressing gown, suddenly feeling very exposed and vulnerable. "Maybe I should get dressed, huh?" She made to go towards her room when Jem lightly grasped her forearm.

"Rachel?"

"It's nothing. Don't worry about it. Once I'm dressed how about I take you out for lunch, I can pick up a Christmas tree and you can give me the gory details on that pole dancing session I missed?" And without waiting for an answer Rachel practically ran to her room. *'Good one Rachel, honestly, 5 minutes in her company and any resolve has bloody disappeared. Pull yourself together woman!'*

* * *

It was just what Jem had needed after a tiring week or so of painting, sanding and lugging heavy beds and sofas up and down stairs. It was a clear and crisp morning. A light dusting of snow the night before had softened up the runs and the skiing was phenomenal. After completing a couple of circuits down the mountain Jem had decided that one final run would clear out the last of the cobwebs, before getting back to reality.

The seat bobbled and swayed gently as the lift hauled the line of eager skiers up the side of the steep hill. Jem smiled sadly as the couple in front of her snapped selfies before kissing, clearly forgetting that everyone behind them could see. '*Ah, to be in love*' she mused, considering her singleton status and the impossible subject of her desires.

As she neared the crest of the hill her phone beeped and she quickly pulled her right hand free from its fleece lined glove. A message from Rachel. Jem quickly typed out a response before smoothly dismounting the ski lift and gliding to a stop out of the way of the other skiers.

Jem zipped the phone back into her pocket, adjusted her goggles and pulled the glove back on before pushing off down the slope, taking a route that veered away to the right. The snow was powdery soft and Jem gracefully curved down the narrow opening into the woods, knocking branches and making little jumps over the uneven ground as the clearing narrowed further. At the bottom of the hill she could make out the dark tan wood of Rachel's cabin, the black pick-up signalling that she was home.

Jem knocked on the door and after a few moments heard the clunk of the deadbolt being released before the door was flung open.

"Hey stranger, what have you been doing? You look like you've been through a snowdrift!"

'Holy fuck, I've missed you' was the only thought that crossed Jem's mind as Rachel stood in the open door. "Hey!" The quiet resolution she had made to take an emotional step back from Rachel evaporated as she stepped into the cabin and threw her arms around the blond, skimming a kiss across her cheek as she pulled her into a close embrace. Jem felt Rachel shudder and saw goose bumps rise over her exposed skin.

"Oooh, you're cold. Come in." Rachel said after a few moments in Jem's embrace.

As Jem took in Rachel's appearance she finally realised that she might only be wearing a thin dressing gown and was suddenly frustrated at the mass of material that had distanced her from the gentle curves she had just being clinging to.

Her frustration only deepened when she spied the obvious reaction to the cold that had Rachel covering her chest with her arms. *'Friends, friends, friends'* Jem reminded herself as Rachel turned and led her into the kitchen, busying herself with the coffee while Jem removed the heft of material that she currently despised. When she finally looked up Rachel was staring, her eyes roaming up and down her body. *'That's different'.* "You okay?"

Rachel just shook her head. "It's just really good to see you."

"It's good to see you too." Jem paused, *'it's time to start the grovelling'.* "Look, I'm really sorry for being an *arse* when you left. There was no need for it. I'm sorry."

"Arse?!"

Jem just smiled sadly, *'I love it when you say that, God I'm in so much trouble. Think 'friends'.* Jem internally chastised.

Rachel looked uncomfortable and began fiddling with her robe, which only drew Jem's eye to the expanse of lightly tanned, flawless skin on her chest, the curve of her collarbone and the hollow at the base of her throat. Rachel began apologising and Jem only just managed to pull her eyes to a more respectable level when Rachel held her gaze with sincere blue eyes that made her fall just a little further.

"Yeah, I don't think it was the shiniest moment of our friendship, for either of us." Jem managed.

"Perhaps not." Jem was pinned by another sincere look. "But it taught me *a lot*…I don't want to lose our friendship. It made me realise how important it is to me…and thinking that you might not forgive me really hit home in an unexpected way."

"What do you mean?" *'Taught me a lot? Unexpected ways? Am I reading too much into this? I am reading too much into this. Probably.'*

Rachel continued to fidget and then made an excuse to escape. All Jem could do was watch her retreat.

* * *

Once Rachel was dressed they took a quick detour back into Bradely, so that Jem could change, and then headed out to Kolton where they could both do their shopping. During the drive and through-out lunch they chatted about what had happened while they were away.

Rachel remained fairly quiet so Jem filled her in on all the big stories about the job, the flat, Thanksgiving and the fateful Tuesday club meeting with the pole! The fog around them seemed to lift as Rachel let out a full belly laugh and then giggled uncontrollably as Jem described how Mrs Alveston, a rather limber 84 year old, exposed the rather snug fitting gold hot pants, mounted the pole and then continued to gyrate her hips before executing a full 360° rotation and perfect dismount.

Rachel's face glowed and she continued to chuckle as she took Jem by the arm and led her out of the restaurant. "God, thanks, I really needed that."

"You're welcome. I love it when you laugh." *'Damn'*. "I thought you were gonna spit your diet coke all over me at one point!" Jem quickly covered.

"I think you had a lucky escape!"

After the women had successfully purchased a Christmas tree for Rachel, a new bathroom unit and mirror for Jem, along with a large soft rug for the living room, Rachel directed them to an art shop where she proceeded to buy, what seemed to Jem, to be copious amounts of paints.

"I didn't realise you painted Rach?"

"Yeah, a lot actually." Rachel said absently as she packed and then paid for her supplies. As she reached the truck she added. "In fact, I've got one that I painted for you as a present for Thanksgiving. Maybe you could find a wall for it in your new flat…if you like it that is!" Rachel was careful to keep her tone even to disguise her nervousness. *'Is this really a good idea?'*

"Thanks, I'm excited to see it. What kind of stuff do you paint?" Jem asked as Rachel pulled 'The Beast' out of the car park, the branches of the Christmas tree, which the girls had carefully tied down on the back, gently tapping on the roof above them.

"Well, as you can see from the paints, I'm pretty colourful. I used to do a lot of landscapes, but recently I've been a bit more abstract. In fact, the one I painted for you was inspired by you." Rachel held her breath for a moment as she casually dropped the new information on the unsuspecting Jem. *'If I do it a bit at a time it might not seem too shocking. Maybe she will work it all out. Then it will be out there, without me actually having to say the words.'*

"Really, no way?!"

"Yep, totally. I could drop it off tonight if you like?"

"Yeah that suits me. You could stay for dinner and help me put it up if you like?"

Rachel shook her head and then looked determinedly back at the road. "No thanks. I've got a script I need to read through tonight, oh, and the Christmas tree to put up."

"Oh? I thought you were taking a break from acting."

"Well, I was, but I got a script through for some voice over work for an animated movie and it looked too good to miss. Plus I don't have to go back to LA to record if I don't want, so that's a bonus."

"Cool. What's it about?"

After swearing Jem to secrecy Rachel talked her through the story line and her character, testing some accents and voice styles out while Jem laughed and evaluated them honestly for her friend.

"I think you've nailed it with that one! Sounded just like I imagined you would as a science genius's super mouse sidekick!"

Rachel chuckled just as she pulled the truck to a stop in front of the shop where Mike appeared and helped Jem lift her new furniture from the flat back of the pick-up. Once everything was unloaded Jem waved Rachel off. "I'll see you tonight and I'll show you the flat then. Are you sure you won't stay for something to eat?"

"No thanks...Besides my painting is a 'love it or hate it' kind of thing...It might not be what you would expect from me, so I'd rather give you chance on your own to decide what you think, without any pressure. You know what I mean?"

'Ah, that's why she doesn't want to come, she's nervous'. "Okay, but I think you are worrying too much."

Rachel simply smiled. 'Just you wait Jem, you have no idea.'

Chapter 9

On arrival Rachel perched the large square package, wrapped in brown paper, by the front door before Jem gave her the grand tour.

"Jem, it's lovely…that roll top bath is fabulous…and I love the polished floors, really gives it a lot of character."

"Thanks, I tested the roll top for the first time yesterday and it was pretty amazing, especially after all that painting!"

Rachel chuckled. "I'll bet…and you did this all in just 2 weeks?"

Jem nodded proudly, rubbing the toe of a socked foot across the smooth, varnished floor.

"Well, that's amazing. I would offer to help if there was anything left to do, but I can see you're all sorted." Rachel smoothed her hair absently before seemingly shaking herself mentally into gear and strode across to the front door where she retrieved her warm down jacket.

"Hey, don't you want a drink before you go? I promise I won't peek at my present." Jem said to Rachel's retreating form.

Rachel turned and tugged her wavy blond strands from the collar of the jacket and shoved her hands into her pockets. "I'd love to, but I really need to look through that script."

Jem sensed that Rachel was making an excuse, but seen as though Rachel was no doubt still recovering from her travels, from which they had pretty much no contact, it all seemed a little too fresh. Jem was determined not to screw up the renewal of their friendship, even if she did want more. At the end of the day Jem knew that she and Rachel had a special bond and she had absolutely no desire to damage or break that.

"Okay, next time?"

"You bet."

And with that Rachel made a hasty retreat, the uncharacteristically nervous disposition making Jem even more curious about the painting. She immediately picked it up and began slowly revealing the artwork as she carefully peeled off the brown paper.

It was as Rachel described. A range of vibrant colours, but these morphed from blackness on one side where a bird, which was mainly white, but flecked with greys and blues, looked to have emerged. It was flying through broad, confident strokes of greens and yellows that gave way to warmer ambers, reds and pinks. The paint was textured and raised off the canvas adding another dimension to the imagery.

Jem perched it on the sofa and stepped away to get a better view. It was incredible. The intensity of the painting had her transfixed and with each glance of the eye she captured a new aspect. After a few moments she focussed upon the bird. It was clearly in motion, but what captured her was the red emanating from its chest, leaving a stain down its body. *'A bleeding heart? Wasn't this meant to be inspired by me?'* On that thought Jem looked at the painting a little more objectively. A bird flying from the dark, into bright colours, reds and pinks no less, with a bleeding heart. Then she noticed the signature at the bottom, it wasn't what she expected. L R Davies. *'No fucking way!'*

Jem sat on the armchair that was positioned at a right angle to the sofa and looked at the painting. Rachel was L R Davies. She couldn't believe it. She had Googled the artist after seeing some pieces at the cabin and had been surprised at the value, but not the gesture. A piece by this surprisingly anonymous artist cost a small fortune, but all the revenue was donated to a kid's charity based around art. Jem wasn't surprised that Rachel would buy art that gave to charity, but it had surprised her how much money she must have invested, based on the amount of work she had in her living room. It made sense now why she had so much by the same person.

Jem swirled the tipple of cherry brandy in a cut glass tumbler and pondered. *'That was why she didn't want to stay. She wanted me to know she was L R Davies, but she didn't want to have to tell me outright.'*

Jem paced in front of the leather sofa before her eyes resettled on the painting perched on the arm. *'But what about the meaning of the painting? It was inspired by me? Really...a bleeding heart?'*

Jem took a gulp of the burning, sweet, syrupy liquid and angled her head to try and see it from a different perspective. It wasn't working.

Eventually she threw herself onto the sofa and pushed her head back against the cushion. *'You know what, she can tell me what this painting means. I'm just not objective enough when it comes to this woman. Why does she have to be so cryptic? What is she afraid to tell me?'*

Having only had a few gulps of brandy, Jem grabbed her down jacket and headed out into the cold, dark night.

***

Rachel sat and watched the lights on the Christmas tree twinkle as she sipped on a large glass of rich, full bodied red wine, the flavours coating her tongue and warming her insides as the alcohol began to take effect. Her eyes flicked lazily across a script as she began to relax and her mind edged away from the nervous fluttering that had set in since she had dropped off the painting at Jem's a few hours ago. *'Red wine, I love you!'*

Rachel's serenity was disturbed by the distinct noise of a vehicle coming up the track. Rachel sat up quickly, placing her glass on the coffee table and the sound abruptly stopped, only to be replaced with the muffled sound of footsteps approaching the front door. Rachel held her breath and an unexpectedly soft knock, followed by a familiar voice doused the momentary worry of a stranger on her doorstep.

"Rachel, it's me. Can I come in?"

Rachel let go of her held breath, only to release the fluttering of thousands of nervous butterflies into her stomach. *'This is silly, I'm a bloody actress. I've been naked in front of complete strangers, yet I'm scared to open the door to someone I care about. Get a grip Clarke.'* And with that quick internal pep talk completed Rachel got up off the sofa.

"Coming." Rachel unlocked the deadbolt and held the door for Jem who was rubbing her hands pensively, looking cold, if not a little anxious. "Hi."

"Hi"

"I thought you were coming in? It's freezing out there tonight." Rachel encouraged as a cold draft wrapped its icy fingers around her shoulders.

"Sorry." Jem manoeuvred around Rachel and went to stand in front of the fire, warming her hands.

"Can I get you a drink? I've got a bottle of red open."

"Thanks, a glass of wine would be lovely."

Rachel poured Jem a glass and gave it to her before resuming her position on the sofa and taking a healthy gulp of the liquid courage. Jem did the same before shedding her jacket and taking a seat at the opposite end of the sofa, her body facing Rachel who was lit by the ambient amber glow from the fire. They looked at each other for a moment before Rachel conceded.

"Did you like the painting?"

"No, I didn't like it." Jem said deadpan. Rachel sucked in a breath and held it, quietly trying to appear unaffected. Jem noticed and then continued once she saw a reaction from the actress, who knew how to wear a mask like the best of them. "I loved it." Jem acquiesced.

Rachel audibly released her breath and then gave Jem a mock glare. "You did that on purpose, didn't you?"

Jem responded with a soft chuckle. "Just wanted to know how much wine you'd had and how well you were wearing that mask of yours tonight."

Jem's honesty cut to the heart of it and Rachel again failed to disguise her response. "Wow! You're cutting to the chase tonight."

Jem simply nodded. "Who knows you're L R Davies?"

"Okay, no small talk then! Let me see, Mum, Sarah and Jack, Matt and Pete and Faye, who works with the galleries and leads ACC…and now you." Rachel shrugged as she held the glass of wine to her chest with both hands.

Jem simply nodded, before adding "Thank you." Rachel looked perplexed and Jem continued. "For trusting to tell me. For being such a generous and talented person. Just, thank you." Jem shrugged her shoulders and was quiet for a few moments. "I'll say it, just in case, I won't be telling anyone." Rachel gave a small smile before talking another large mouthful of the delicious red wine.

They both sat in companionable silence, enjoying their drinks, until Jem broke the quiet with a whispered question. "What does it mean Rach? The painting?"

Rachel placed her glass on the low coffee table and looked into the fire, her thoughts still swirling as her desires fought admirably against her pessimistic view on the reality of being a celebrity. "Do you really need to ask?" She replied in a hoarse whisper, laced with emotion. Desires were winning.

"No, yes, I don't know!" Jem threw up her arm, nearly sending the red wine sloshing over the rim of the heavy crystal glass, so she placed it on the table before shaking her head. "I don't know anything about art, what if I'm misinterpreting it?" *'If I'm wrong I'll put our friendship in a really awkward position.'* Jem looked carefully at Rachel who for the next few minutes remained resolutely transfixed by the fire.

"I don't think you'll be wrong." Rachel finally turned to look in Jem's eyes and then held out her hand and placed it gently on her knee. Rachel's heartbeat thudded so loudly in her chest that she though Jem would be able to hear it too. *'Oh my goodness, I'm really doing this! Please let this be right.'*

Jem placed her hand over Rachel's and gently clasped it in her own. She could see the pulse on Rachel's neck and a flush of colour rise up her chest into her cheeks. Jem slowly shuffled forward, maintaining eye contact, as she tentatively leaned forward and hovered her lips over Rachel's.

It only took a moment, but time seemed to stand still, before Rachel closed the distance and placed her mouth onto the full, soft lips of the brunette in front of her.

The kiss was tender and gentle as lips tasted, properly, for the first time. But as certainty grew Jem deepened the kiss, brushing her tongue across Rachel's lower lip. Rachel sighed and opened her mouth allowing Jem to explore and tongues to entwine in a sensual dance. Jem released Rachel's hand and ran her palms slowly up both arms, onto her neck, before entwining one in her hair and the other gently caressed Rachel's cheek. Rachel leant forward, holding herself up with one hand on Jem's thigh and the other at her waist.

This was a far cry from the passionless kiss at the bowling alley. Jem's heart swelled and the ache of desire settled into all the usual places. Eventually Jem retreated from the kiss and placed both hands onto Rachel's jaw and looked carefully at the woman before her. Rachel's eyes fluttered open, the blue just a narrow rim around wide black pupils.

"I could kiss you forever. Your lips are so soft." Rachel lent forward again and captured another swift kiss. *'Oh my, this is so right.'*

Jem just sighed with contentment. "Is this what you wanted?"

Rachel bit her lower lip, before leaning forward, capturing Jem's face between her hands and whispering "Yes" against her lips as she engaged her in another heated kiss. As Rachel increased the intensity she leaned her weight onto the slightly shorter woman, pushing her back against the armrest of the sofa, effectively closing any gap between them.

After a few intense moments the kiss slowed from frantic to deeply sensual and Jem couldn't resist slipping her hands under the chunky sweater, looping them around Rachel's waist and then up the warm soft skin of her back.

After a moment, Jem found a resilience she didn't know she had, removed her hands from Rachel's back and gently pushed her away. Both women were breathless with slightly swollen lips, confirming the intensity of the kiss.

"Wow!"

"You're telling me. If I'd known kissing a woman was this good I'd have done it years ago!"

Jem simply smiled, reached for the glass of wine and then seemed to think better of it, replacing it onto the coffee table as she stood. "I'd better not drink any more or I won't be fit to drive…You want a cup of coffee?"

Rachel looked at the wine and knew that drinking more would only cause a shadow of doubt over what they had just done. "Yes, please."

As Jem busied herself with making the coffee, Rachel sat at the dining table, watching her friend move confidently around the kitchen. *'She's such is a beautiful woman'* Rachel mused, only to be found staring by Jem who held a steaming mug in front of her, a small smile curling the corners of her lips.

"Thanks." Rachel beamed in response, knowing she had been caught looking.

"Soooo…you want to tell me about it?!" Jem sat in the chair opposite and blew on her coffee before taking a tentative sip while waiting for Rachel to formulate a response.

"Well…I suppose I always found you attractive, but it took Rick to open my eyes."

"Rick?!"

"He was being such a chauvinist prick, and, well, I don't know…When I kissed you, I didn't think, and I gave you my best practiced Hollywood effort. But then, it just felt…empty." Rachel shrugged and focussed on her coffee mug before continuing. "And then you were so angry and I knew I'd messed up. It felt shit. Shittier than I thought it would…and when I painted it out, well, some emotions I hadn't realised I had came forward. Seeing Pete helped, and having the distance to see it, to see you…" Rachel looked intently at Jem before continuing. "It just, well, shed some light onto some dark areas for me."

"Well, I suppose I'd better thank Rick!" Jem joked, trying to lighten the levity that had settled over them.

"I was frightened." Rachel added unexpectedly, her voice barely above a whisper. She looked away for a moment to compose her features before returning her gaze to see the concerned look on Jem's face. "I didn't know how you felt about me, and I really didn't want to jeopardise our friendship. I care about you deeply and I don't want to do anything that might hurt you, ever."

"Oh, Rachel. Geez, do you know you?! I tried so hard not to be attracted to you, to distance myself from that. But you are so kind, thoughtful, fun, generous and, well, to be blunt, gorgeous." She joked as she waved a hand in the direction of the woman across from her.

Rachel simply smiled gently, shook her head and murmured a "thank you" before taking a long drink from her mug.

Jem quickly finished her coffee and stood. "I should go. I'll see you tomorrow?"

"Yeah, that would be good." Rachel stood and faced Jem. "Do you have a busy day?"

Jem took a tentative step towards Rachel. "Not too bad."

Rachel mimicked Jem, leaving a small gap between their bodies. "Maybe I could make you some dinner?"

"That would be lovely. What time do you want me?"

"Whenever suits you. I'll aim to serve dinner at 7ish?"

"Ok." Jem leant forward, gently holding Rachel's slim waist as she tracked small, soft kisses from her cheek across to her lips, where she landed a soft peck before pulling away. Rachel let out a shaky breath and Jem used what remained of her will power to grab her coat and give a small wave before disappearing out of the door into the brisk night.

As her SUV trundled down the track and pulled onto the main road she spotted a grey sedan tucked into the roadside. A man's face was partially lit from a phone which was being used to illuminate what looked like a map. *'City folk, I hope he's got snow tyres on!'*

Chapter 10

"Why was I not informed about this sooner?" Rachel huffed as she tried to reign in her temper, *and fear*.

"Ms Clarke, we have tried to make contact with you on several occasions, both in writing and over the phone. I'm sorry these have not reached you."

Rachel cast her eye over the stack of mail she had picked up while she was back in LA and quietly cursed at her lack of PA. In truth, she didn't want to share her personal life with an employee and had vowed to remain grounded, despite the wealth and fame she had amassed during her career. She let out a shaky breath. "When did you lose contact with him?"

"He failed to register for parole 2 weeks ago. We've put out his details and officers are aware and on the look-out. However, we've had no sightings since issuing the BOLO... as yet."

"2 weeks!" Rachel felt her heart rate increase and a panic seize her chest.

"Yes Ma'am. I understand your concerns. Now we know your location we have informed the local law enforcement agencies. Please remain vigilant and take the necessary precautions. I realise from your previous experiences with Mark Copland that you are well aware of the type of precautions to take?"

"Yes Detective Winters."

"You have my number and the local PD's, please use them if you have any concerns."

"I will." Rachel responded quietly, her mind whirling with the repercussions of this simple phone call.

"Ms Clarke?"

"Yes?"

"As soon as I have any further information or news I will be in contact."

"Thank you." And with that the call ended. Rachel remained motionless on the sofa, her calm exterior contradicting the turmoil within.

Dinner plans with Jem were the last thing on her mind. The knock on the door sent Rachel cascading in a heap from the sofa, knocking the air from her body while simultaneously causing her heart to pound a frantic beat.

"Rachel? Are you there?"

Rachel immediately recognised Jem's voice and jumped to her feet, flinging the door open. Grabbing Jem's hand she tugged her into the cabin, slammed the door shut and flung her arms around the slender, yet solid frame of the slightly shorter woman. Rachel buried her face into the side of Jem's neck and began sobbing.

"Hey!" Jem's posture softened after the initial, unexpected, barrage of blond. "What's up?" Jem's tone was soft, matching the gentle and reassuring rub of her hands up and down Rachel's back. The pair stood like that, in the growing darkness of the room as dusk fell, for what seemed like an age until eventually Rachel's tears eased and her breath evened out. Jem gently leaned her head back to look at the tear stained cheeks of the woman she adored, worry painting her features, as she assessed Rachel's emotional state. In a slightly more authoritative tone she asked Rachel again. "What's going on Rachel?"

Rachel's sad blue eyes held Jem's. "He's back."

Jem searched Rachel's face again. "Who? Who's back?"

"Mark Copland, my stalker."

It didn't surprise her that Rachel had a stalker, she was beautiful and famous, surely a recipe for such a thing. "How do you know?"

Rachel led Jem to the sofa, sitting so close their thighs touched from hip to knee. She held Jem's hand between both of her own, gently stroking it as she explained who Mark Copland was.

"It started about four and a half years ago. He was a fan. Apparently I'd signed a photo for him at an appearance." She looked briefly into Jem's eyes. "I don't even remember, there are always so many people at these things and you sign literally hundreds of the damn things." A sigh escaped and she looked back at the entwined fingers on her lap. "Anyway, things escalated over time. He was always hanging around, not just near the studio but places I'd go, like the grocery store and the dry cleaners. At first he didn't approach, but then he started to talk to me and would ask me out and stuff. Obviously I refused. I tried to let him down gently, but after that didn't work I was firmer about it." She shook her head. "It didn't deter him, just seemed to make him more determined." Rachel gave a little shudder and Jem instinctively pulled her into her side and draped an arm over her shoulder. Rachel lent into the embrace, her head tucked into the crook of Jem's neck. "I got the Police involved after he became more insistent. I got a restraining order, which seemed to help for a while, but in truth I think it just fuelled him to be more devious." Rachel looped her arm around Jem's waist and held her tighter. "About a year after it all started I started publicly dating Matt. I thought it would help. It's part of the reason our agreement developed. We were both helping each other out, just not in a way that people think…I've never been attracted to a woman…until now." Jem said nothing, just pressed her lips to Rachel's hair, gently encouraging her on with her story, amazed that she had no idea about any of it. "Well, after we announced our engagement, he totally disappeared. I was so relieved. Living in a state of being hyperaware, paranoid really, was exhausting. Well, when we got back to LA after the wedding and 'honeymoon' I spotted him. He'd shaved his head, grown a beard, lost a ton of weight…it didn't matter, he'd hounded me for the best part of a year, either up close or from a distance, I would have recognised him anywhere…his walk gave him away." She shook her head. "A bow legged gait!" Rachel chuckled mirthlessly and leant further into Jem and took a deep breath, allowing the scent to envelop her. Jem just held her tighter, she could feel Rachel becoming more anxious, her shoulders slowly morphing into rigid plains of tense muscle. "He tried to kidnap me…they found his van. He was going to hurt me…he'd planned and prepared for it…it was sick Jem, sick."

"Shhh, I'm here." Jem gently whispered while wrapping her other arm around the slightly trembling body.

"He went to prison. Got 2 years, served just over 14 months." Rachel shook her head, as if trying to get her brain to process the new information. "Detective Winters called this morning to say he's been missing for the last 2 weeks. Failed to meet or make contact with his parole officer…I think all the news of Matt and I getting a divorce might have set him off again." Rachel let out a shuddering sigh and whispered. "Jem, I'm scared."

Jem simply held tighter to the trembling mass, rocking slightly, whispering reassuring words into her hair. "I'll stay here with you tonight. But, maybe you could stay with me in town?…Hardly anyone knows you're here. How could he possibly find you?"

"I don't know, but he's clever Jem. I've always been really private and even more careful when he was watching me. But when he was at his worse he would always show up at a restaurant or even at a secret meeting place with Matt or my friends. I don't know how he did it."

"Do you want to come to mine tonight?"

"NO! I don't want to go out in the dark. Will you stay with me tonight? Please."

The fear in Rachel's voice was obvious and Jem acquiesce without any further encouragement. "Of course. Let's get cosy." Jem slipped from under Rachel's body and flicked on some lamps, quickly drawing the curtains and double checking the locks on the door and windows as she went. Satisfied these were all in place she loaded the fire before putting on the kettle and puttering in the kitchen.

Rachel sat and watched with wide eyes, arms protectively wrapped around her stomach as Jem loaded the low table in front of the sofa with meats, cheeses, crackers and any other tasty bits and bobs she had found whilst rummaging in the fridge and cupboards. She poured some tea and a good snifter of brandy for them both.

"Let's watch a movie." She announced once the smorgasbord of food had been laid out before them.

"Okay."

Jem rummaged and found an English movie she had never seen amongst Rachel's collection. "Four weddings and a funeral?"

Rachel forgot herself and chuckled. "Whatever you want."

The pair snuggled up on the sofa, a blanket draped over them. Both were relaxed after eating their fill and drinking the brandy, the once hot tea now cold and untouched. When the credits finally rolled across the screen Jem stretched and yawned. "Well, that was very, ah, English!"

"Gotta love Hugh!"

Jem stood in front of Rachel and held her hands out, gently tugging her off the sofa and leading her to the bedroom, switching off the lights as they went. When they arrived Jem pulled Rachel into a tight embrace, their bodies touching from where their cheeks pressed against each other all the way to their knees. "You okay?" Jem whispered into Rachel's ear before lightly placing a soft kiss below the lobe.

"As long as you're here." Rachel replied as her body gave a soft shiver from Jem's contact, encouraging her body to somehow meld further into Jem's.

"I'm not going anywhere." Jem gave another soft kiss.

Rachel exhaled before softly brushing her lips against Jem's cheek and tentatively onto her full lips. Jem softly returned her kiss before pulling away slightly. "We don't need to do anything tonight. Let me just hold you, make you feel safe."

Rachel responded by whispering "okay" onto Jem's lips before deepened the kiss, her tongue gently exploring and beginning to entwine with Jem's. Jem could feel desire pool at her core. Rachel was making love to her mouth and she was finding her resolve to resist eroding, especially as Rachel's hands made their way up her sides to caress her back and then the undersides of her breasts. Jem pulled away slightly and took hold of Rachel's hands.

"Let's get some PJ's on." She wanted to take it slow, Rachel's day had no doubt been an emotional rollercoaster and she didn't want to rush her into something she wasn't ready for.

The two women shimmied around each other, changing into pyjamas and using the bathroom, until eventually they were tucked snuggly under the thick down duvet. They lay, facing each other, with barely inches between them, but neither one touching the other.

"You are so strong, you know that?"

Rachel shook her head. "I don't feel it."

"How come I never heard about this?"

Rachel released a deep sigh. "I'm a private person Jem, I really didn't want this getting out. The LAPD were really fantastic."

"Why didn't you tell me?"

"This is all part of a past I just wanted to forget. It made me stronger in some ways, but in others it affected how I interact with people. How I trust people. I know I can trust you. You're so honest. You treat me like, well like me, and not some movie star. Honesty like that isn't so easy when you're in the spotlight the whole time…it's why I love it here in Bradely. I can just be me."

"I'm not always honest."

Rachel searched Jem's eyes, which despite her words, seemed only to communicate understanding and honesty. "What do you mean?" Rachel breathed.

"I'm your friend, but if I'm honest…I think I've been attracted to you since the first night I spent with you at the cabin…that's not how a friend should be."

Rachel blinked slowly before responding. She leaned forward, mere millimetres from Jem's lips. "If I'd had any sense I would have realised that too. I knew you were different, I just hadn't connected the dots in my head."

Jem could feel Rachel's breath on the damp of her lips and closed her eyes, hoping for some injection of strength that would help her survive the night without ravishing the vulnerable woman before her. Clearly Rachel was having none of it. She closed the minute distance between their mouths, brushing her tongue across her lips, seeking an invitation to deepen their contact. Jem allowed the kiss to unfold for a few moments before gently pulling her mouth away while enveloping Rachel in a tight embrace. Without any words they lay together until eventually sleep quietly stole them away.

Rachel slammed her back against Jem, her breathing laboured and her arms and legs were kicking out against the duvet.

"Rachel...Rachel, wake up, it's just a dream." Jem tentatively rolled and pressed herself against Rachel's back and gently placed an arm around her stomach, while continuously whispering reassurances into her ear. Rachel's movement eased and a hand moved to rest over Jem's as she slowly awoke from her nightmare.

"Sorry, did I wake you?" Rachel whispered.

"It's okay. Did you have a bad dream?"

Rachel shuddered involuntarily and shuffled backwards so that she could feel Jem's body enfold her even more tightly. They stayed like that until the dark of the early hour was chased away by the rising sun and the nightmare had become a distant memory.

The feeling of Jem's body pressed against Rachel's back had ignited a small flame of desire that grew the longer they lay together. Rachel began gently stroking Jem's hand with the pads of her fingers, slowly extending the movement up her forearm and then onto her upper arm. Rachel registered the slight hitch in Jem's breathing which encouraged her to scrape her short nails back down the length of the warm arm embracing her. This triggered a wave a goose bumps and the release of a long shuddery breath that tickled Rachel's ear. Rachel did it again, this time Jem nuzzled into the crook of Rachel's neck before trailing soft kisses from her shoulder, up the slope of her neck to just below her ear, a particularly sensitive area, which made Rachel release a low quiet moan.

As if petrol had been thrown onto the flame, Jem increased the intensity of the kisses on Rachel's neck, gently moving the spaghetti strap of her camisole that she slept in, revealing new flesh to lavish with her mouth. Rachel entwined her fingers with Jem's and placed them against the soft warm skin of her belly before moving their joined hands to cup her full breast.

Moans filled the room and Rachel leaned her head to one side, trying unsuccessfully to connect her lips with Jem's. When this failed she rolled in the confines of Jem's arms and captured her mouth in a searing kiss, fuelled by the desire generated from the hand that was gently kneading her breast and clamping down on a sensitive nipple.

"Jem" Rachel moaned into Jem's lips as she released her hand and brought it round to grope Jem's buttocks, trying desperately to bring her into closer contact with her now writhing body.

Keen to feel the warmth of Jem's skin against her own she trailed her hands up, tugging the hem of Jem's tank top up and over her head. The break in contact between their lips allowed Rachel's eyes to feast on Jem's breast. "Perfect" she whispered before lowering her mouth over a nipple.

The movement caused Jem to roll onto her back, allowing Rachel to lie between her legs, her mouth and hands worshipping the dark pink buds while she pressed her weight against Jem's need.

"Oh God, Rachel." Jem exclaimed as she bucked her hips against Rachel and reached her hands down under the soft material of her pyjamas to cup the warm, soft skin of her firm backside.

Hands became frantic as they both fought to remove the material barrier between them, while lips and tongues plundered mouths in a sensuous dance that replicated the movements of their bodies. Once naked their bodies writhed against each other frantically until Jem took the lead and rolled Rachel onto her back, holding her hands loosely above her head.

Looking down she could see the desire in her lover's face, her chest heaving, with a light sheen of sweat covering her glorious body. Jem lent down and kissed her so tenderly, so reverently that Rachel began to still. Jem held Rachel's gaze before peppering soft kisses down her slender throat, dipping her tongue into the hollow at the base before continuing lower to lavish her breasts with nips and licks that had Rachel arching her back off the bed, moaning loudly. Encouraged by the sounds of Rachel's pleasure Jem opened her mouth wide and suckled deeply on her right breast, rubbing the flat of her tongue rhythmically over her nipple while she pinched its partner firmly. Rachel clasped onto Jem's head and held her tight against her chest as a wave of pleasure rushed over her, causing her to tremble and cry out.

Jem continued to knead and pinch Rachel's breasts with her hands as the orgasm claimed her, as it did Jem's mouth trailed southwards. After dipping her tongue into Rachel's naval she looked up, locking blue eyes to brown. Never breaking contact Jem lowered herself further and positioned Rachel's legs over each of her shoulders. Rachel's chest was heaving, the remnants of her orgasm leaving her with a slight tremble and a flush of colour that extended up her throat and across her cheeks. Dipping lower she parted Rachel's folds and kissed her tenderly in her most sensitive place. Rachel let out a shuddering sigh and closed her eyes, breaking their eye contact. Jem focussed on the task at hand, determined to make this the best Rachel had ever had.

Jem licked and suckled, her hands reaching around to massage her backside firmly and rhythmically in time with the movements of her mouth. When she could feel the quiver of Rachel's need she raised her buttocks with one hand while dipping her tongue and then thrusting two fingers into Rachel. It was all it took for Rachel to fall off the edge. The orgasm washed over her in waves that gripped onto Jem's fingers, causing her body to stiffen and tremble while she cried out incoherently. Jem continued to thrust and lap, extending the pleasure until Rachel lay limp and rung out.

Rachel threw her arm across her eyes. "Oh my goodness, you're unbelievable."

Jem cleaned herself up on the sheets before kissing her way back up Rachel's body, coming to rest on her side to admire the celebrity's perfect profile. She laid her lips lovingly on Rachel's cheek and splayed her hand across the firm naked abdomen. After a few moments Rachel turned to face Jem. "Hi."

"Hi" Jem responded almost shyly.

Sensing Jem's shyness she leaned forward, her fingers brushing over Jem's lips before she followed with her tongue. Jem took in a shaky breath and that was all the prompting Rachel needed to realise that Jem was probably still wired and needed her own release.

Rachel's intrepid fingers felt their way over Jem's chin, down the valley between her breasts before coming to rest on her hip. "So beautiful." Rachel breathed against Jem's lips before holding her gaze with an intense look that communicated the desire and longing she felt. Jem gave a slow blink as Rachel nudged her onto her back. Positioning herself above her lover, Rachel kissed Jem tenderly, pouring all the love she had for this woman into that one action. When they were both breathless Rachel pulled away, again eyes locking as Rachel parted Jem's legs to nestle against her, hip to hip, breast to breast. Rachel began moving against Jem who wrapped her legs around Rachel's hips, their needs pressing and rubbing against each other. Rachel brought her right hand down to caress Jem's butt before moving it around to press a finger, then another, tentatively at first into her channel. Jem took a sharp breath, but never broke eye contact or the sure and steady beat they were creating between them. Rachel could feel her desire building again as she continued to thrust herself firmly against and into Jem. She was grappling to retain her control when she felt Jem pulsing against her fingers, her breath quickened and then finally her eyes closed as she bucked up erratically against Rachel and gave a long breathy moan. Jem pressed herself firmly against Rachel's clit and hand, extending her pleasure and causing Rachel to fall with her.

Rachel lay limp on top of Jem, her face buried in her neck as they both steadied their breathing. After a few minutes Rachel delivered a tender kiss before untangling herself so they lay facing each other, conscious of her weight pressed against her lover.

Jem swept her hand up Rachel's thigh and looked her directly in the eye, communicating more than words could. Rachel smiled shyly before taking in a deep breath as Jem continued to stroke her thigh, moving round to lightly caress her backside.

After a few minutes Jem shuffled slightly closer, their mouths just an inch apart, their breasts brushing lightly. Jem continued her gentle caress, light fingertips tracing patterns up and down her back, across her butt and down the tops of her thighs. Rachel let out a shuddering breath as, to her surprise, her libido reawakened and desire caused her eyes to close. This allowed her senses to focus on Jem's fingertips, which were becoming bolder and had ventured down her arms and were now creating a trail of goose bumps as they snaked a path over her breasts and around nipples, that were already sensitive from the earlier adoration they had received.

Rachel's breath hitched and Jem claimed her mouth in a searing kiss, deep with sensuality as tongues moved rhythmically against each other. This felt more intimate than before, and despite making love just a short time ago, neither woman could resist the temptation to touch and feel. It was a sensation overload and Rachel could no longer remain passive, her hands cupped and fondled Jem's full breasts while she hooked a leg over Jem, searching desperately for some friction to ease the throbbing between her legs.

Sensing Rachel's urgency Jem rolled her weight over her and pressed her into the mattress before lifting her upper body up on her forearms. Brown eyes found blue as Rachel continued to caress Jem's breast while Jem reached round to pull Rachel's legs up over her hips. They rocked into each other, Jem raising Rachel's hips off the bed to push closer against her. Breathing became more stilted and heat ignited their intertwined bodies. Jem reached down into Rachel's slickness, pressing the flat pad of her thumb against her clit and filling her up with her fingers.

"Ahhh, Jem…Jem, oh fuck…oh my Goodness, I'm gonna come." Jem reached up and pinched her nipple firmly and Rachel moaned loudly, her body convulsing wildly as Jem extracted an earth shattering orgasm that left Rachel boneless and panting beneath her.

"Fuck Jem, holy fuck!" Rachel wrapped her arms around Jem's neck and pulled her close until her heartbeat calmed back into a steady rhythm. Jem tried to move her weight off Rachel, but Rachel clung onto her more tightly. "Stay here, I love the feel of your body against mine." They fell back into an exhausted sleep.

Chapter 11

The shrill ring of an old fashioned phone broke the calm of the bedroom, disturbing the steady breaths of the sleeping occupants. Rachel suddenly sat up to attention, like she's just been zapped by a bolt of lightning and dragged in a lungful of air. Her hair stood, all dishevelled and mussed up from their nocturnal activities.

"Phone?!" Her voice was rough from sleep as she escaped the bed on wobbly legs and began hunting around for her phone, eventually locating it under the bed in a pair of discarded trousers.

"Hello."

"Good morning, is this Rachel Clarke?" It was a smooth, deep voice with an American accent.

"Whose calling please?"

"This is Detective Reynolds from the local Police Department. Is Ms Clarke there?"

"Yes, that's me."

"Good morning. Can I just confirm a few details before I go any further?"

"Yes, of course." Rachel replied as she rubbed the sleep from her eyes and pushed the tangled mane of hair out of her face.

"Please can you confirm your address and date of birth Ma'am."

Rachel rattled off the details, eager to discover if any progress had been made with her stalker.

"Thank you Ma'am. This call is regarding Mr Mark Copland. The Detective in charge has requested that I collect a written statement regarding the circumstance of this case."

"Oh, okay."

"Ms Clarke you are welcome to come down to the station to make this statement or alternatively I am up near Bradely this afternoon and we can complete it in the comfort of your own home. Which would you prefer Ma'am?"

"Thank you for your consideration, please could we do it here at the cabin? What time suits you, sir?"

Rachel heard a heavy breath down the line, which was quickly drown out by shuffling and the clanking of a spoon against a cup. "Well, I'll be in the area this afternoon. Is 4pm convenient for you?"

"Yes, that's fine thank you Detective. I'll see you this afternoon."

"Thank you for your co-operation."

Rachel ended the call and turned to look at Jem, who was rubbing the sleep from her eyes. *'How cute.'*

"That was Detective Reynolds, he's coming by this afternoon at 4pm so that I can make a written statement."

"Okay, good to see they're taking it seriously."

"Yeah." Rachel lent down a placed a tender kiss on Jem's mouth. "You at work this morning?"

"Shit, yes! What time is it?"

Rachel quickly checked her phone. "It's 10.25"

"Fuck!" Jem scrambled out of bed, grabbing clothes off the floor as she ran into the bathroom. "I've got a lesson at 11am and I need to get my ski gear from home." With that she disappeared into the bathroom, emerging a few moments later with her trousers half done, top on and a toothbrush poking out of her mouth. Like Rachel her hair was like a birds nest at the back.

Stifling a laugh at the dishevelled brunette. Rachel inquired. "I'll see you tonight?" Jem nodded as she rinsed the toothpaste from her mouth.

"Yep. 6.30 pm at mine and then onto Gram's for Tuesday club. Christmas crafts and mulled wine." Jem wiggled her eye brows as she said 'mulled wine', indicating what Rachel already knew - it would be a drunken evening.

"Right, I'll be there."

Jem lent down "Or you'll be square!" She placed a quick kiss on Rachel's mouth and lovingly smoothed her blonde locks behind her ear before dashing out of the bedroom. Moments later Rachel heard the thud of the front door closing and the hum of Jem's car. Rachel flopped back down onto the bed and considered the events of the night. "Wow, who knew?" She said quietly to herself.

* * *

A dark grey sedan pulled up and a man with a Stetson, which shielded his face from the sun reflecting off the snow, exited. As he walked up to the cabin the steel of a gun flashed in the sunlight as he adjusted his coat and the police badge, which was clipped to his belt. Rachel watched him from the window and then moved to open the door. He had a long handlebar moustache and sandy blonde hair, but there was something familiar. Rachel felt the hair on the back of her neck stand to attention as realisation hit, but before she could slam the door he wedged his foot against it and forced it open. Rachel stepped backwards to create some distance between them, but he hitched his jacket around to reveal the gun in the holster cradled on his side.

"Hi Rachel, long time no see." The voice morphed from the smooth, deep all-American accent from the phone to a more familiar, slightly higher pitched one with a southern twang that had haunted her.

Rachel was stunned into silence, adrenaline and fear coursing through her. She stepped back into the dining table. He took this opportunity to close the distance between them, his bow legged gait now obvious as he walked confidently, dominantly, towards her.

He removed the gun from the holster in a slow and deliberate movement, then pressed the barrel against the underside of her chin and lifted her face to meet his. Rachel turned away from the cold grey eyes and his hot breath, that held the distinctive scent of whiskey. He leant forward and licked his tongue all the way up the right side of her face, leaving a trail of wet saliva that made her blood run cold and an involuntary shudder ran through her.

"I missed you. All that time in prison gave me lots of time to think. Now you're a single lady again I figured it's my turn." He rammed his hips against hers and rubbed against her suggestively as he continued. "That queer was never good enough for you." He leaned forward and smelled her hair in a predatory way and Rachel held her body tense and still, like the hunted prey she was. "Yeah I saw, I heard. You need a real man."

His cologne combined with the stench of whiskey was overpowering, causing her nostrils to flare. But her body remained rigid and taut, leaning away from him as best she could as he continued to crowd her, pushing her firmly against the table.

Whilst he held her trapped he took another opportunity to mark his territory by running his snake like tongue up her neck to her ear sloppily. She shuddered, repulsed by his action. With the gun barrel still tucked under her chin, he reached a hand around his back and pulled a set of hand-cuffs from yet another clip on his belt.

Rachel's eyes widened, the fear unmistakable in her eyes. "You don't need those." Rachel pleaded. "I'll do what you ask."

"Then you'll wear them or I'll make it worse for you." He said in a sing song voice.

He pushed the gun more firmly against her neck, causing her to mewl in pain as he grabbed one of her wrists. He stepped away slightly, lowering the weapon as he applied the cuffs roughly, binding her wrists across her stomach. The metal clasps were tight and bit into her flesh.

He gave the links between the cuffs a hard tug to before slapping her hard across the face. Rachel lost her balance and fell heavily on the polished wooden floor, her cheek tingling from the force of the slap, her shoulder and hip aching from the heavy landing. "That's for denying me. I won't let you do that again."

Rachel felt the tears rise in her eyes and the shake in her muscles as the adrenaline raced through her. She inhaled a shaky breath and rapidly tried to blink the tears away, desperate to put on a mask that would hide the fear gripping her as her worst nightmare became a reality.

Roughly he hauled her up from the warm, smooth wood floor using the handcuffs, which caused the skin to welt and hot pain shot up her arms and down to her fingertips. Rachel bit her lip as she stifled the cry, stubbornly remaining quiet, in an attempt to refuse him of any pleasure he might gain from overpowering her.

Despite his gait he strode across the room, pulling her forcefully down the stairs outside the cabin, where she lost her footing, tripped and landed on her knees in the driveway. The gravel from the road shredded her skin causing her knees to bleed, the small sharp stones embedding themselves into her kneecaps.

With one hand still holding onto the links between the cuffs and the other clenching the gun, he popped the boot of the grey sedan. Rachel could see where this was going. Her breathing accelerated and her attempts to resist took on a more frantic edge, as she writhed and twisted, scuffling and skidding on the loose chippings. A fine sheen of sweat was visible on his brow and his large Stetson fell to the ground as he grappled with her eel like movement as Rachel tried with all her might to escape her captor. Rachel flailed, her foot making a heavy contact with his shin and he cursed loudly.

"Fucking bitch. You'll get in this fucking car or I'll fucking make sure it doesn't end with you. You understand." He snarled.

Rachel felt like she has just been sluiced with ice water as she interpreted his words. *'It won't end with you.'* Oh no, not Sarah and the kids. Rachel stilled and he let go of the cuffs and pushed the gun into her lower back, forcing her into the trunk before slamming it with excess force, not caring if she was low enough in. The trunk thwacked onto her head and she blinked against the explosion of pain, holding in her cry as the darkness of the confined space enveloped and imprisoned her. Her ears filled with a loud ringing, the searing pain in her head was excruciating, unbearable. The light lunch she had consumed a few hours earlier ejected itself from her stomach in sharp convulsions that forced her into a tight ball. One hand held her cramping stomach while the other slipped against the slick liquid that oozed from the crown of her head. Warm liquid ran down her chin before another kind of darkness claimed her as she slipped into unconsciousness.

Rachel blinked groggily into the darkness. The ringing was not as loud, but the pounding of pain in her head continued, matching the still frantic beat of her heart and intensifying every time the car jolted over a bump in the road. Time had eluded her but she could hear the rumbling of the tyres on a tarmac road below and the motion of the car, indicating that they were still driving. *'Where is he taking me?'*

She shivered uncontrollably from the cold, which seemed to have permeated her bones, and fear, the weight of which was pressing heavily onto her chest, making it hard to breathe. *'Perhaps I could just stop…then I wouldn't have to go through any more.'* As soon as this thought filtered her aching head she knew it wasn't an option. *'What about Sarah and the kids? What about Jem? He can't hurt them too. It has to end with me.'*

After what seemed like an eternity the car stopped, the hum from the engine died and then a door slammed, the sound reverberating off the inside of her skull causing her to close her eyes tightly against the agony it magnified.

Rachel curled up tighter, the action causing the matted hair and dried blood and vomit on her face to pull her skin taught, exacerbating the sharp pain in her head. She closed her eyes and mentally prepared for the trunk to open, but all she could hear was the crunching of footsteps in the snow slowly fading into the distance. The cold ran its icy fingers down her spine and her shivers became more violent as any mild warmth that had leaked from the car faded.

Chapter 12

Jem looked at her watch again and knitted her brows in concern. *'It's after 7 pm and Rachel said that she would meet me at 6.30 pm so that we could go to Lucy's together.'* She tried the mobile again, but it just rang out. Jem left yet another voicemail before hopping into her SUV and driving up to the cabin. *'She might have just got absorbed in her painting and not realised the time'*, Jem reasoned with herself in an attempt to calm the feeling of unease that had settled over her. But no matter how much she tried thoughts of Rachel's stalker and the fear on her face last night kept haunting her attempts at rationalisation.

When she arrived at the cabin it became apparent Rachel wasn't there. The cabin was in darkness, except for the intermittent blinking of the Christmas lights which, given the circumstances, threw an eerie multi-coloured glow out of the windows.

Jem walked up the steps and tried the door. To her surprise it opened. Alarm bells were ringing soundly now as she tentatively entered the cabin, calling out and switching lights on as she went. When there was still no response. Jem moved more frantically through each room of the compact cabin, calling and then listening intently. But everything was eerily still and quiet. The fire had burned low and there was a cold, half-drunk cup of tea on the kitchen counter.

Jem couldn't stop the shiver than ran through her as she hastily unlocked her phone to ring the Police. For the next 10 minutes she was transferred from one department to another, where she relayed her story. No-one had ever heard of a 'Detective Reynolds' which seemed to eventually trigger a call to Detective Winters. He seemed like a man of few words, but despite this he had an air of authority and confidence about him. Jem was instructed to wait and not touch anything, prompting her to hastily stuff her hands into the pockets of her jacket.

As she waited Jem looked more objectively at the cabin and noticed the salt and pepper lying on their side on the dinner table and the rug had been tugged, making the coffee table sit at an odd angle to the fire and the couch. A cold, leaden feeling sank to the pit of Jem's stomach and she began counting her breaths as she waited impatiently for the cops to arrive.

Half an hour later Winters arrived along with other officers who carefully navigated their way into the cabin. Detective Winters was a tall, lean man who looked to be in his late 40's. She was right, he had an aura of confidence and authority that surrounded him like a force field. As he walked up the gravel drive Jem could see him pointing at areas on the path, firing out instructions to tape and then photograph places where the gravel was scuffed. Jem moved out onto the porch and Detective Winters nodded a quick greeting before continuing to observe the surroundings. Under the intense glare of a strong hand held search light, blood encrusted bits of gravel shone damply. Jem swallowed the lump in her throat and fought the urge to vomit.

Eventually Winters instructed Jem to sit and proceeded to scribble notes into a compact battered black leather notebook as she relayed the few details she knew about the meeting scheduled with Reynolds at 4pm. Just before they finished Jem remembered the grey sedan from the other night. "It was probably just a tourist checking his route, but it was late and it's not a particularly busy road. It looked grey, but it can be hard to tell sometimes in the dark. It wasn't a local plate, that's another reason I figured it was a tourist." Jem recalled hesitantly.

"We've had a possible sighting yesterday but we're still following this up. It could be nothing." Winters said, briefly looking up from his notes. His deep voice and professional demeanour gave nothing away causing the tickle of panic to turn into a hollow pit in her stomach.

The feeling of powerlessness washed over Jem, making her slump back into the sofa like a rag doll. Her emotions threatened to overtake her and she could feel her eyes filling. "What happens now?"

"We'll put an APB out, get these prints confirmed ASAP and take it from there. If you hear anything please give me a call immediately." He passed his card to Jem who fisted it into her pocket. "For now I want you to go home. Stay by your phone." His voice remained steady and professional, but his eyes warmed as he looked at the bewildered and frightened young woman before him.

Jem gave Detective Winters Lucy's address and shakily made her way out of the cabin to her truck. Once ensconced behind the leather steering wheel she allowed the tears to silently cascade down her face as she drove, on autopilot, back into town. Her thoughts were immovable from the woman whom she had recognised for the last 10 years, but had only really known for a couple of months. Despite this Rachel had reached every corner of her consciousness, had monopolised her thoughts and had set up residency in her heart.

When Jem pulled in front of Lucy's house she could see the swarm of bodies through the steamed up mullioned windows. Jem heaved herself from her SUV and made her way up the freshly shovelled and gritted path along the side of the house. The smells of Christmas wafted from the house and punctuated the air, igniting a wave of nausea that Jem hastily swallowed down.

Lucy was stirring a vat of mulled wine, the alcoholic steam wafting in swirls around her as she stirred the burgundy liquid that was being gently heated on the stove top. She smiled warmly as she sensed Jem enter the room, but one look at the face of her granddaughter and she realised something was wrong. The smile slipped from Lucy's lips and her face contorted with worry, creating creases she rarely wore on the soft skin of her forehead

133

and around her lips. Lucy dropped the wooden spoon with a clatter and quickly enfolded Jem in a warm embrace by the back door. Jem's pale complexion and trembling body spoke volumes.

In the safety of Lucy's arms Jem began sobbing and through sniffles and hiccups relayed the pertinent parts about Rachel's stalker and the events of the last 24 hours. Clearly in shock, Jem began to shake and Lucy placed her granddaughter in the tall rocking chair next to the stove before hurrying into the living room to dissipate the crowd. Jem could hear Lucy talking but all the words were lost on her as she closed her eyes and began gently rocking. On each forward move she whispered a short prayer or request to whatever deity would listen.

* * *

"You're back early."

Linda shook a few stray flakes of snow off her woollen jacket as she made her way over to the bar where her husband finished pouring a drink and placed it in front of Rick, who was perched on a leather clad stool at one end.

"Oh God, you wouldn't believe it. Rachel's gone missing and the Police think some psycho stalker has done it."

"What?" Both Linda's husband and Rick said in unison as they gave her their undivided attention, Rick's movement stalled as he held his glass halfway to his mouth.

"Yeah, I know. Apparently some guy was stalking her years ago and went to prison. A complete nut job by the sounds of it." Linda said as she twisted a bar cloth in her hands, a nervous habit that revealed the angst she was experiencing.

"Poor Rachel, no wonder she likes Bradely so much."

"Well, she did until he found her." Linda stopped for a moment, her face paling as she considered what Rachel could be going through, revealing the shock that such a tremendous thing could happen in such a small, close-knit community. "We've been asked to be on the lookout. If I tell you two what they're looking for you can ask as many people as possible if they've seen anything, yeah?" Both men agreed, looking serious as they absorbed the information to share.

Rick looked perplexed for a moment, before slowly repeating the information back to Linda. "You say a grey sedan and walks weird, like he's been sat on a horse too long?" Linda nodded at the slightly distorted, but still accurate description she had given. "A fella like that booked Ma's cabin. I had to plough the snow so he could get his vehicle up. He's been here 3 days, booked for another 4."

"Really? You sure?"

Ricked nodded confidently. "Definitely, wore a big Stetson and a handle bar moustache. He almost looked comical with that get-up and his bowed legs." Rick said shaking his head, a grim look on his face as he finally let the frost glass of frothy beer finish the journey to his lips. After taking a deep draught of the amber liquid he swiped the residue from his top lip and looked at Linda. "Call Jem now." But as he said it Linda already had the cordless phone pressed to her ear. Jem picked up before the first ring had even finished.

Chapter 13

Rachel's legs were numb from the awkward position and the cold, which seemed to have penetrated to her core, making her sleepy. Just as she thought she might die of hyperthermia the trunk opened, jolting her awake and causing a fresh bout of pain to radiate from the contusion on her head.

It was dark, all but for the light leaking through the open door on a small cabin. The windows were blackened, no doubt by thick curtains designed to keep the cold out.

Mark grabbed her shoulders and roughly yanked her from the trunk, flinging her to the floor unceremoniously. The uneven ground connected with her cheek as she landed awkwardly, unable to save herself due to her stiff, cold limbs and the handcuffs that joined her hands in a tight grip at her front.

"Get up bitch!" He slurred loudly.

Rachel lay prone on the ground and he placed a swift kick to her stomach. She couldn't hold in the groan, despite her best efforts to remain mute and blank featured. With some difficulty he lifted her up and pushed her face down onto the back of the sedan and leaned over her, his erection pushing against the back of her legs.

"Maybe I should take you here? Perhaps you like being fucked up the ass…married to a gay." He barked in disgust before he shook his head, as if in disbelief. But the action caused him to wobble and sway slightly, the alcohol affecting his co-ordination. "What do you think, eh?" He whispered drunkenly into her ear, spraying her with saliva across her cheek causing her to close her eyes tightly and swallow down the bile that was rising up her throat.

She could hear the rattle of his belt and the sound of a zipper being released, but her fight was gone, still heavily winded from the kick to her midriff. She heaved air into her lungs, trying desperately to catch a breath. "You won't be able to see what you're missing, but you'll fucking feel it." He spat into her cheek, the pungent smell of whiskey invading her senses.

Tears slid down her cheeks as he leaned back and pinned her to the car with his hips, undid one handcuff and yanked her arms around her back before swiftly re-cuffing her, still so tight that her wrists burned as the steel dug into the already bloodied and bruised flesh. Rachel gritted her teeth and swallowed the pain in her shoulders as he yanked her hands down roughly. He put the gun on the back of the trunk and began tearing at the button of her jeans. With a new surge of adrenaline Rachel lent into the car as much as she could, kicking out with her legs, throwing her head around trying to butt him, despite the violent complaints from her brain, which was rattling around painfully in her skull. She writhed and thrashed her torso too, trying to make his task as difficult as possible. She let the mask, she had been so carefully keeping in place, fall and let all of her fear and hurt out in a series of incomprehensible screams. She expelled all the air in her lungs to make her voice as loud as possible, in the hope that someone, anyone, might hear her cries for help.

Copland, who was struggling against the flailing woman, yanked the chain of the handcuffs roughly and swiped a backhand in the direction of the face that was being thrown violently against him. Rachel let out a sharp yelp as his hand connected with her cheek and ear.

Suddenly there was a hell of a noise and it took Rachel a moment to realise it wasn't her. People were shouting angrily as they seemed to emerge from the dense woodland surrounding the cabin. Spotlights illuminated the area and Rachel leaned her head forward against the cold metal of the trunk, exhausted and relieved, as Police yelled warnings at her kidnapper. Copland pressed his front against Rachel's back, surreptitiously reaching for the hand gun. More orders were barked aggressively from the

137

surrounding officers as Copland made a swift, but ultimately drunken, final grab for the weapon and pointed the swaying gun at his captive. Rachel squeezed her eyes closed, waiting for the inevitable.

An ear-splitting shot rang out.

A moment passed and Rachel opened her eyes, expecting some out of body experience, a calling to a bright light or something that signalled the end of this mortal life. But to her surprise she was exactly where she was before, except she was no longer being pressed against the cold metal of the trunk of the car, instead the figure of her abductor lay prone on the floor, his eyes glassy with a stain of blood leaking onto the front of his pinstriped shirt. The flash of light from a spotlight reflected off the brass police badge on his belt drew her eyes away from the rapidly pooling blood that looked black against the stark white of the freshly fallen snow.

When Rachel blinked there was a woman at her side. She had a gentle, reassuring voice as she laid a blanket across her shoulder. *'Thank God they came when they did.'* A sob escaped, and realising she could cry she let all the hurt flood out of her.

Chapter 14

Jem ran down the long white corridor, skidding into the door frame as she approached the room.

Rachel was laid in the bed, her eyes closed. Her right cheek was purple and had a series of abrasions across the width of it. She had a bandage wrapped around her head, failing to hide the matted, bloodstained locks of blond hair. Her skin had lost its golden hue and was as pale as ivory. Her features were relaxed in sleep and she looked like a beat up china doll in the bed.

Gently Jem sat on the edge of the bed and tenderly brushed some of the long blond wavy hair from her face. Rachel lazily opened her eyes and Jem could see her scanning the room and then gazing, glassy eyed and unfocussed at her. "Hi." She slurred.

The nurse had said she was heavily medicated, she had a concussion and extensive bruising with minor cuts and scratches. *'Injuries we can see, what about in that beautiful mind of hers?'* Thought Jem.

"Hi." Jem leaned down and very gently placed a kiss on the edge of Rachel's mouth, away from the bruising of her right side.

Rachel sighed. "Sleepy."

"Okay, you sleep."

"Don't go, stay with me." Rachel pulled her hand from under the covers and grabbed hold of Jem.

Holding in a gasp, Jem responded as evenly as she could. "Don't worry, I'll be right here." Rachel's wrist was a shade of angry red and purple with weeping welts that were already beginning to scab and bruise around the whole circumference.

Whilst still holding Rachel's hand she reached for a chair and sat as close as she could. She stroked her hand gently, soothingly, as Rachel's breathing became deep and even again. She swept her lips over her fingers before laying her cheek on them as she silently cried out her relief and anguish. Her tears fell freely as she considered the haunting experience Rachel had just endured and the 'what if's' that kept unwillingly filling her head in surprisingly high definition.

Jem realised she must have dozed a little, as she was jolted awake by a ruckus in the corridor and the bedroom door swung open. Jem blinked the sleep from her eyes as she saw Rachel, followed by another slightly older blonde lookalike jog into the room. *'No that wasn't right, Rachel was right here'*, her hand still held in her own, their fingers intertwined loosely. That must be Sarah and her Mum. Rachel wasn't kidding when she said they were identical twins. *'I wonder how that feels not to be totally unique, aesthetically anyway?'* Jem pondered that idea for a millisecond before her thoughts crashed back into the present as the two women looked critically at Rachel, then Jem and then their entwined fingers.

"Hi, I'm Jem, Rachel's friend." Jem reluctantly released Rachel's hand and gently placed it on top of the covers before offering an outstretched hand to Sarah.

"I'm Sarah and this is our Mum, Louise." Sarah directed an outstretched arm to the older lady who was now on the opposite side of the bed to Jem, stroking her daughter's hair and kissing her forehead while whispering quiet reassurances into her ear. A stream of tears was plotting a course down her cheek, which she hastily swept away with the back of her free hand.

Jem stepped away from the bed and Sarah took her place, holding Rachel's other hand. Rachel cracked an eye open, then the other. "Hi" she rasped sleepily.

"Oh Rachel!" Louise lifted one hand to her lips and smoothed her hair back lovingly with the other. Silent tears slowly started down Rachel's cheeks and Sarah smoothed them away.

"Hey there big sis!"

"Hey there little sis. How are the kids?" Rachel asked, her voice still hoarse from earlier.

"They're fine, more concerned about you right now." She spoke quietly, her eyes warm and crinkled with worry.

Jem found the mirroring of their faces disconcerting, like live walking and talking before and after models.

As Rachel became more cogent she took in the small space, her eyes searching and then stilling when they landed on Jem who had retreated to the back of the room. Sarah and Louise noticed. "You met Jem?"

"Yes darling, she's been keeping you company. Jem, come and pull up another chair." Louise gestured her across.

Once they were all settled into seats they began discussing everything and anything other than the events of the day. It was well into the early hours, and after Rachel had fallen back to sleep, when Sarah and Louise finally persuaded Jem to go home and get some sleep. Jem was reluctant, however she didn't want to intrude, so slipped away.

After making the half hour journey home she swiftly showered and changed then nipped to Rachel's to grab some clothing, her phone and a couple of bits and pieces to make her stay in hospital as comfortable as possible, before making the journey back in record time.

Jem arrived in at 6.30am to find Rachel sleeping and both her sister and her Mum talking in hushed voices.

"Hi, I brought Rachel some things back from the cabin, to make her more comfortable. How has she been?" Jem whispered.

"Mainly sleeping, I think those pain meds have really knocked her out." Sarah said as she lightly rubbed her thumb across the back of Rachel's knuckles. "We were just talking to the doctor, who popped in to do a check-up before the shift change, and she seemed to think that she would be allowed out this evening."

"Oh, that's good I suppose. You're always more comfortable at home that in a noisy hospital being prodded and poked all the time." Jem responded cautiously as she swapped the bag of Rachel's belongings nervously from one hand to the other.

"Yes, but we're not sure how Rachel will feel about going back to the cabin." Sarah shared a worried look with her Mum and Jem. "We were wondering if we should take her back to Portland with us."

"Oh, right." There was a moment of silence before Jem re-found her voice. "But perhaps staying here will keep her out of the limelight. I'm sure she wouldn't want this being discussed in the media. She could stay with me, or perhaps at my Grandmother's house…She has a large house and you are all welcome to stay while she recovers." Jem took a steadying breath and licked her lips before adding. "Of course, if that is what Rachel and you guys want?" Jem said looking hesitantly between the two women who were eyeing her with a certain amount of, *'what was that, curiosity?'*

Suddenly a hoarse whisper interjected. "If that is okay with Lucy I would really like that." Rachel gently cleared her throat, temporarily scrunching her eyes shut, as though the action had caused a mini explosion in her head. "I really don't want the media getting hold of this and I feel like Bradely is my home. I don't want to be anywhere else right now."

142

Jem, who was stood at the end of the bed, gently rubbed Rachel's foot over the covers and smiled at her. "Whatever you want." She replied, holding in the 'my love' that she wanted to add to end of that statement.

The next 12 hours seemed to pass at a snail's pace. Both Sarah and her Mum, Louise, seemed surprised at Jem's attentiveness to Rachel. Obviously they were completely unaware of the fact that their relationship had morphed from friendship into something more romantic in the last 48 hours or so. Jem had rarely left Rachel's side, instead she encouraged Sarah and Louise to go to Lucy's in the late afternoon where they could change and sleep before she was released, arguing that they didn't all need to be there to bring her home and they would be better placed to welcome her back at Lucy's well rested, with the house prepared for the patient.

When they finally left, after much fussing, Rachel breathed a sigh of relief and beckoned Jem to her side. "Hi"

"Hi, how're you doing?" Jem asked gently.

"Better, heads clearing a bit."

"You happy about the arrangements?" She hadn't wanted to ask in front of her family, she didn't want to cause any trouble. In fact, she felt like she had been walking on eggshells the entire day, not wanting to seem overly affectionate or obtrusive in front of Rachel's nearest and dearest.

"Yes. Come here." Rachel beckoned for Jem to come to her. They entwined their hands and Rachel gently tugged Jem closer. "Come real close, I need to whisper something into your ear." Jem lent forward so that their cheeks brushed lightly. "Thank you." Rachel placed a gentle kiss just under Jem's ear, then on her cheek. As Jem lent back slightly Rachel placed a soft kiss on her lips.

"You're welcome." Jem whispered against her lips before tenderly returning her kiss, relieved that Rachel still wanted her like this.

The sound of the door being opened caused Jem to quickly retreat, creating a more socially acceptable distance between them, as Sarah dashed in.

"Handbag! Honestly I'd forget my head if it wasn't screwed on!" She reached under the plastic chair and grabbed the black leather bag, quickly straightening. "I'll see you soon at the house, okay?" Rachel nodded before Sarah laid a quick peck on her cheek, she then nodded and smiled at Jem and left.

"Do you think she saw?" Rachel asked Jem while she worried her lip with the finger from her free hand, the other still entwined with Jem's.

Jem looked at their joined hands for a second before looking at the worried expression on Rachel's face. "Nah, I'd moved back before she'd even got through the door." She squeezed Rachel's fingers. "Are you worried about what they would think?"

Rachel shrugged and fidgeted with the bed covers, letting go of Jem's hand. "No, I think Sarah would be fine, Mum I'm not so sure. Either way though, we've only just, ya know, so I thought it would be better to see how it goes…I've been told that I have my flaws, so I didn't want you to feel pressured or anything…Plus, if the media gets wind of it, there'll be no peace and I wouldn't want to subject you to that."

Jem simply nodded and was about to respond when the Doctor and a nurse entered the private room. After a final assessment Rachel was given strict instruction to rest and take it easy for at least the next 3 or 4 days and was given a prescription for some paid meds.

Rachel gingerly got dressed, clearly a bit stiff and sore with what she described as "a bit of a headache" that was clearly bad enough that every time she moved her head too quickly she stopped and squeezed her eyes shut. Nevertheless she fixed on a smile and thanked everyone as they left, waving off Jem's help saying "I'm fine, honestly." *'Yeah right'*, she wasn't fooling this one.

After a very careful drive home, with Jem avoiding all potholes and bumps in the road, they eventually got Rachel to Lucy's and settled onto the generously sized overstuffed sofa in the large double fronted living room. Rachel was tucked under a soft fleece blanket and the fire crackled reassuringly, sending a warm amber glow across the room. This combined with the delicious smells of beef stew wafting from the kitchen caused Rachel to sigh contentedly, snuggle more deeply into couch and close her eyes.

Jem stood in the doorway and observed the contentment on her lovers face. Gram had gone all out to make her guests feel welcome. Jem had barely been able to hold in her gratitude, engulfing her Grandmother in a warm hug as she stood in front of the stove, smiling proudly at the pot of bubbling beef stew and dumplings she had just extracted from the oven. She had made it in homage to the Clarke's English heritage and as a gesture to welcome the house guests that Jem had thrust upon her with hardly any notice.

'God, Gram is one in a million.' Jem thought as relief and pride flooded through her.

Chapter 15

The fire blazed, the lights on the Christmas tree twinkled and the chatter flowed as the women acquainted themselves with each other. Despite looking exactly alike it was apparent that Rachel wasn't lying when she said they had different personalities. Sarah had a fantastically dry sense of humour and quick wit that set her apart from Rachel's easy going, slightly cheeky persona. As a combination Jem could imagine they would make quite a double act. As it was, concussion and all, Rachel was laid out on the sofa with her head on Sarah lap. Sarah absently plaited lengths of Rachel's long blond hair between sipping her wine, laughing and sharing stories about their childhood in England with Lucy and Jem.

As the evening began to draw in and coffee had replaced the wine, a loud knock on the door shattered the peace. Jem rose to her feet quickly, placing a gentle hand on Lucy's shoulder to prevent her struggling to her feet from her favourite bottle green leather armchair, from which the colour was worn and the leather soft from overuse.

"I'll get it. It's probably just the Police." Jem padded to the door in her stockinged feet and glanced through the peep hole. All she could see was the back of whoever was at the door. Sighing she released the latch and opened the door. As soon as she did a bright light shone into her face, momentarily blinding her. Looking down she noticed that the woman in front of her, who was wearing a sharp blue suit, was thrusting a microphone in her direction while someone with a camera cradled on their shoulder, bright light attached, stood facing her.

"Hello I'm Carrie Williams reporting live for CBN news. Is Rachel Clarke here?" The woman blinked expectantly while Jem stared blankly at the camera before a flash in the background and another minivan pulling up, drew Jem's eye to the street where several vehicles were parked and several photographers and news crews were making their way up to their door. Carrie Williams continued, clearly needing to fill the dead air space. "Is it true she has been abducted?" She paused, allowing Jem to answer, which she did not. "...Can you confirm that she is still alive?...Has her abductor been captured?...Did she have a stalker?...Is this anything to do with her divorce from gay action star Matt Franks or his partner Pete Coles?" The questions never stopped and were like machine gun fire as Carrie hurled them at the startled brunette in front of her.

It took a moment, but the situation finally seemed to be registering with her slow, sleep deprived brain. Jem knew better than to answer any question and slammed the door and turned to face Lucy, Sarah and Louise who were stood, mouths agape, in the hallway. Clearly she wasn't the only one shocked with the speed in which the press had picked this one up.

"Shit!" Sarah said in a loud whisper.

"How on earth?" Louise began pacing in the corridor and Jem leaned her back against the door. Suddenly a flash of white light seemed to reflect off Sarah's white top.

"Fuck!" Sarah dashed into the sitting room where Rachel was. The curtains were only partially drawn. A few photographers had their lenses pressed against the glass and Sarah rushed to tug the heavy curtains shut. This blocked the lenses but not the name they were calling or the questions they were shouting.

Rachel, who was pale before, now looked even more shaken and ghost like. Clearly she was in no position to deal with any of this, so Sarah took the lead. "Lucy could you and Jem check that all the doors and windows are locked and the curtains closed. I can't imagine they would come in, but let's just be certain that they can't." Lucy and Jem nodded before setting about their task.

Sarah turned to Louise. "I'll call Sandy Mum, if you call the Police and tell them what's happening. They may not be able to help us, but it's worth notifying them." Louise nodded and then began rummaging in her oversized handbag as Sarah continued. "I'll call Matt after I've talked to the Police. He should hear from us rather than seeing it on TV…*Shit,* I should have called him sooner." And with that Sarah jumped into action, looking for her phone and frowning at the screen that lit up her features as she hunted for the correct contact details.

While Sarah and Louise talked on the phone Jem paced listlessly. *'How the hell did the press know anything about this? Who could have leaked it?'* An obvious suspect came to mind, she just hoped she was wrong. Escaping to the privacy of Lucy's bedroom upstairs, Jem angrily stabbed at a number in her phone.

"Hey babe. Ringing to thank me for finding that psycho?" Clearly now the shock and panic had died down he had recovered his confidence. *'Yep, Rick was definitely still a sleaze.'* Jem thought as she sighed at his welcome.

Holding in her anger Jem answered in the sweetest, most even tone she could muster. "Oh yeah babe. That was awesome of you. Thanks. Did you tell anyone else about your sleuthing?"

"Eh, sleuthing? What's that?"

"Ya know, about finding the guy?" Jem answered, struggling to maintain the casual tone of her voice.

"I may have toasted my awesomeness in the bar." Rick sniffed, clearly proud to boast to anyone within earshot.

Jem's tenuous grasp on her temper slipped. "Rick you fucking idiot! The press is here hounding us. What were you thinking?!"

"Errrr, I dunno. What do you mean the press?" Rick stumbled, clearly taken aback by Jem's sudden change of tone. The earlier cocky confidence he had exuded evaporated. "Those lads at the bar wouldn't do that." He replied shakily.

"Really. So you don't think the promise of a few hundred bucks could loosen their tongues?"

Rick's silence said it all. Taking in a deep breath Jem brought her voice to a more palatable level, so not to startle the rest of the house again. "Did you tell them about what happened at the bowling alley?"

"Fuck no!...Wouldn't want them thinking that I couldn't bag a babe like you." He said in a quieter tone.

Jem's hand shook as she rubbed her forehead. It would appear that Rick's bravado had at least saved Rachel from being 'outed', but this whole series of events was hard to stomach and she felt the pressure behind her eyes build as a headache developed at a rapid rate. "Okay. Rick? You can't talk to anyone else about this. Please? This is so messed up right now and Rachel doesn't need this."

"Okay. Look I'm sorry. I never meant for that to happen…I didn't even think about that."

Rick was still a nob, and clearly the source of the leak, but to Jem's surprise, he sounded sincerely sorry about it. Letting out a sigh, she finished the call. "Okay. Bye."

Once Jem had returned to the living room Sarah was finishing up her call with Sandy. They had constructed a brief statement to the press. A couple of Officers from the local PD had also arrived, but it was apparent that there was little they could do to remove the press entirely. Jem looked across to Rachel who was sat on the sofa, an oversized baby blue cotton shirt engulfed her, making her look vulnerable and a little lost. Her eyes swept across the statement Sarah and Sandy had written over the phone. Her jaw was set firm and she rested her head at a slight angle on one hand, like it was too heavy to stay up by itself. Once she had finished reading she talked briefly to Sarah who scribbled a couple of extra notes onto the paper before dashing off to talk to Louise.

Seeing an opening Jem approached, sitting herself gently down next to Rachel. "Do you want to watch this upstairs? There's a TV in the spare room." Rachel nodded and looked down at her hands, which were now clasped in front of her, the sleeves of the oversized shirt covering the welts on her wrists. "Okay."

Jem rose and offered Rachel some assistance, but rather uncharacteristically she avoided the possible physical contact and rose slowly to her feet before shakily exiting and climbing the stairs to the small, but cosy spare room.

They waited quietly, hearing the statement being read out to the waiting press outside. Sarah spoke clearly and confidently through-out, wavering only once when she said that Rachel was safe and would make a full recovery. However, her tone took on a firm edge when she requested that it was essential that the media stepped back while Rachel recuperated from her injuries and the Police completed their inquiries.

A barrage of questions were hurled at the pair once the statement was complete, but they refused to answer. On re-entering the house they came up to the bedroom where Jem was perched on the side of Rachel's bed, both glued to the small TV screen to watch how the new channels were spinning it.

After observing the story unfold on several main channels they'd seen enough, it was the same information and shocked responses just read out in slightly different ways. Rachel had turned deathly pale and was eerily quiet. On seeing Rachel's appearance Louise ushered everyone from the room, but as Jem turned to leave Rachel caught her sleeve, giving it a light tug before quickly releasing her.

"Can you stay a moment?" Rachel asked, looking at the door where the others were.

"Sure." Jem looked at the pale features of her friend and lover. The abrasion on her cheek contrasted starkly to her fair complexion, but what surprised her was the downward tug of her lips and the dullness in her eyes that displayed a level of emotion she had never seen before.

Jem averted her eyes and caught Sarah's, who was looking from one to the other. She gave a brief nod and a sad smile that seemed to say that she understood. It occurred to Jem that twins had more of a connection than just their looks.

When the door clicked closed Rachel let out a deep sigh, then said "Jem, we need to talk."

Chapter 16

Jem rose to her feet and pulled her hand away from Rachel's. With each backward step she felt the leaden weight of dread increase in her stomach. "Is this what you really want?" Jem asked in a hushed, anguished voice she barely recognised.

Rachel shook her head while she softly answered "Yes."

Clearly her words and her body language were at odd with each other so Jem asked again, more forcefully. "Are you sure you want this Rachel?"

Tears leaked down Rachel's face, across the swollen and scabbed cheek. "Yes!" Her words matched Jem's in force but again Jem hoped the tears weren't lying.

"What if I love you?" The slight waver in Jem's voice was the only indication of the emotional turmoil that was unfolding within her as she held her jaw firm and her body rigid.

Rachel looked away for a moment and set her features in a way that suggested to Jem that the mask was back in place. "Then you'd better stop. I'm not for you Jem." Rachel said in a steady, firm tone and then held her tongue before the rest of her thoughts tumbled from her loose lips. *'You're too good for me and the wolves in the press. It would be better for Jem this way.'* In the back of her mind Rachel had known it was wrong to pursue Jem, but being in Bradely lowered her guard and allowed her heart to lead her head. *'How foolish, the media attention around her divorce should have been enough. Matt and Pete having to beat off the press, the gossip and the homophobes should have been enough. Well, a murderous stalker was the final sign and, as they say, third times a charm.'* Rachel thought resentfully as her celebrity status finally caught up to her.

Jem stepped back again to further increase the distance between them as she absorbed the cutting words Rachel had just delivered.

She bumped against the soft pink wall of the compact spare room. Her stance straightened and a pained look fleeted across her face before her features hardened and she mustered the resolve to respond. "I understand." She said evenly, in a voice that went some way in disguising her emotions. "I always knew it wouldn't work. I just didn't want to believe it." With that she swiftly left the room, clicking the door closed softly behind her.

Rachel collapsed back against the pillows and curled herself into the foetal position. The bruise across her stomach ached and her head throbbed, but it was all insignificant compared to the pain erupting in her chest as her heart splintered and shattered. Despite the self-inflicted situation the agony was still shocking and caused her body to heave uncontrollably as the anguish broke free and the dam burst. All of this was exacerbated as the pained look on Jem's face replayed in her mind's eye and joined together in a chilling collage with the other haunting images of Mark Copland and the scenes he had created.

***

After taking a few moments to compose herself in the bathroom Jem made her way downstairs and met Lucy in the kitchen. "Gram, if it's okay with you I'm gonna go home. I didn't sleep last night and I feel wrecked. Will you be okay dealing with all the guests?" If her heart wasn't aching so much she would have felt more guilt at abandoning her Grandmother with all of *her* invited guests, and the uninvited ones outside, who were still milling about in the hope of catching a glimpse of the battered celebrity in their midst.

"Are you sure? I could get the airbed out and you could set up in the study?...What about all the journalists outside?" Lucy asked, concern colouring her features and her eyes scrutinising Jem's.

Oh the guilt, she couldn't live with it. "Sure. You're right. Where's the airbed?" Jem replied, trying to add intonation to her voice to add some cheer, which sounded false even to her own ears.

Lucy gave her another long look before her face softened and she nodded. Either she had fooled her Grandmother or, more likely, she realised Jem was on the verge of an emotional breakdown and needed some space. "It's in the chest in the study." Lucy said once she had turned and began busying herself with the kettle.

Jem moved on autopilot, retrieving the airbed and getting it set up in the study in record time. She threw a sleeping bag on top before going in search of Louise and Sarah, who were talking quietly in the front room.

"I'm gonna turn in. I didn't sleep much last night and I need to lay down before I fall down." Louise and Sarah exchanged quick 'good nights' before Jem scurried off to her makeshift bedroom.

Despite being exhausted sleep eluded her. The heartbreak was settling in now, causing a hollow vacuum in her chest and stomach, all of which left her feeling nauseous, cold and restless. Thoughts of the media camped outside made her paranoid, hushed conversations and the soft padding of stockinged feet up and down the stairs seemed to continue through-out the night. By 5 am Jem gave up and went in search of coffee, hoping it would shake the veil of fatigue and the ache in her head, no doubt caused by the pressure of unshed tears.

To her surprise Louise and Sarah were already up, cradling cups of steaming tea in their hands. Sarah looked so much like Rachel that Jem could barely glance in her direction, so instead she busied herself with coffee while asking the obvious. "You're up early?"

154

"Yeah, we're going get out of your hair good and early. Hopefully, fingers crossed, before too many of those photographers are out of bed." Sarah replied.

"Oh?" Jem tried to hide her surprise. Relief mixed with dread and she concentrated hard on adding milk to her coffee, her backed turned away from her guests. As she stirred in the clouds of white to the strong black coffee she riffled through her emotions and tried not to wear them all on her sleeve as she turned back to Louise and Sarah.

"Yeah, we've been up most of the night. Got a security team arriving shortly with a car and we're on the 6.38am flight back to LA." With that Jem's head shot up and she looked between Louise and Sarah.

"It's for the best." Louise continued where her daughter had left off. "It's not fair to subject you and your Grandmother to all of this… Rachel's house in LA is much more private and should protect her from the photographers."

"Right." Jem gulped down the scalding coffee. '*How in my life did I EVER think this would work with Rachel? She has a house in LA for God's sake.*'

By 5.15am they were gone and the house, which had been crowded with people and swarmed by the media, felt suddenly still, quiet and, in Jem's case, heartbreakingly lonely. The tick of the clock seemed overly loud, as did the shaky breaths that rattled in and out of her lungs as she tried to hold the tears at bay.

'*That's it, it's all done now.*' And with that thought cycling through her mind, as if on repeat, the tears she had held back began to run silently down her cheeks. Jem allowed them to run off her chin and plop unceremoniously onto the floor where she watched them glisten in the false fluorescent glare cast from the under counter strip lights.

Chapter 17

2 months later...

Christmas had come and gone in a haze and before Jem knew it she had taken up her position as a paramedic in the nearby town of Kolton. It was the job she had pursued for the last 3 years, and yet even that had failed to successfully lift her from the doldrums.

When she was on the job she was jovial and professional. She had made a good impression with her new colleagues and made friends in the small, tight knit unit. But as soon as she got in the car, or walked through the door of her flat, her face fell and an overwhelming feeling of loss would engulf her in the lonely apartment.

Having a broken heart sucked and, at this moment in time, Jem had no idea how, or if, it would ever mend.

Although Jem steered well clear of the gossip magazines sometimes it was impossible to ignore the images of Rachel on the front covers and the bold headlines that were splashed around them. Rachel had been photographed as she left Bradely a couple of months ago looking battered and beaten. The images of her hanging her head low with oversized sunglasses on to hide the damage had shocked the people of America and as a result had stirred the talk shows and newsrooms to debate the various issues of violence, stalking and celebrity.

As Rachel shied away the media seemed to grow hungrier for the story. Eventually, a month after she had returned to LA she had done an interview. The criminal case was no longer active and in the interview Rachel professed that she just wanted to 'leave it all behind her'. Since then any images seemed positive, usually of her smiling, out with friends or on set at the animation studio, for what was expected to be the next Pixar smash hit.

Overall every image was like a punch in the gut for Jem, she looked so well put together it made her look and feel like a joke.

'I'm part of that 'leave it all behind' bit. Don't forget that Jem.' Despite her frequent and rather depressing pep talk Jem was still struggling, but trying, to move on. As Gram would say *'time is a healer'*. This was a saying which Jem frequently added to the internal dialogue that constituted a pep talk and, she had to admit, that even though her heart felt like hundreds of shards of splintered glass and her stomach a hollow pit, there were now only hundreds and not thousands of splinters and the hollow no longer felt like it reached her toes, just her knees.

***

Rachel plastered on a smile as yet another paparazzi snapped her walking from the grocery store. Getting in the non-descript silver Prius, the environmentally acceptable car most celebrities seemed to own like some kind of company car, she carefully set down the brown paper bag before pulling out into the stream of LA traffic. She maintained her neutral features all the way back to her LA residence. Once the large wooden gates closed behind her she scowled. "Fucking paparazzi, won't they give me a break?" She heaved the shopping out and stomped up the front steps into the house. She could feel her tenuous grip on her temper slipping as she rammed the groceries away in the refrigerator and various cupboards.

"I need to run!" She mumbled to herself as she stripped out of her loose fitting white shirt as she walked to the bedroom to retrieve her gym kit. Once she was ensconced on the tread mill she gradually hitched up the speed and the volume on the iPod strapped to her arm. Running had always been her thing and once she'd got a few kilometres under her belt she felt the tension start to drain away. But she couldn't stop the direction of her thoughts until she reached the painful part and then remembered she wasn't thinking about Jem. *'Jem who had the softest skin. Jem would had brought her such unexpected pleasure. Jem who she could simply just talk to, without the weight of expectation...Shit! Who would want her crazy life? Certainly not Jem. But I pushed her away. We didn't even discuss it, I didn't even explain myself. Argh...I need to paint.'*

Punching the buttons on the treadmill Rachel eased the pace and began her cool down. She took a quick douse in the shower before pulling on her paint splattered shirt and padded into the studio. Rachel stood square to the easel and assessed the progress on her current piece. She'd never done a portrait before but she was giving it her best shot. Although it may not have been wise to paint Jem it was only thing she wanted to paint, and doing so seemed to transport her, allowing the hollow feeling in her chest where her heart once resided to be temporarily forgotten and filled.

Chapter 18

Enough was enough. *It's my birthday and I am going to get a grip of my life. No more sulking, no more pining. It's time to make myself happy. It's time to move on.* Jem chastised her reflection in the brightly lit bathroom mirror.

- ☐ *Pep talk complete? Check.*
- ☐ *Glad rags on? Check.*
- ☐ *Looking good? Not bad! Just need to find some shoes.*

Jem tucked the a few tendrils of thick wavy brown hair behind her left ear. She'd taken the time to put some volume and curls into her hair and wore it down so that it caressed her bare shoulders, revealed by the silky turquoise halter neck top that clung to her slim figure. After a quick rummage through the haphazard pile of shoes in the bottom of the closet she found a pair of heels that perfectly matched the top and contrasted well with the skinny black pants. She pulled them on and stood before the long mirror attached to the wardrobe door.

- ☐ *Looking good? Check. Check.*

She wasn't out to pull because, let's face it, she was probably the only lesbian in Bradely but Jem was determined to look good for her birthday meal at Linda's restaurant, which was only across the street so she could easily stumble home after she had cashed in all her birthday drinks! This evening was going to be her fresh start and as of 5.17pm she was officially beginning a new year of her life.

When she arrived Jem quickly located Lucy, Mike and Rita who were sat around an oval table decorated with a pale table cloth that sparkled with glitter and gaudy 'happy birthday' confetti. But what really drew the eye was the riot of balloons attached to each of their chairs. Jem smiled genuinely for the first time in over two months. These were her most important people and they had clearly gone to some effort to make her feel special for her 31st birthday, which to be fair, was no significant milestone.

Lucy met her half way and enveloped her in a warm embrace, quickly followed by Rita who proceeded to give a long armed hug, hindered by her gloriously rotund belly.

"I've put money on it being a boy! It's all at the front. When did you last see your feet?!" Jem joked as she rested her palms lovingly across Rita's tummy.

"Hey, I missed you." Rita said as her soft, watery green eyes found Jem's.

"What, you only saw me last week?" She said over Rita's shoulder as the very pregnant lady engulfed her in another tight hold, taking Jem by surprise.

"I know, but you look good tonight." She leaned away, holding Jem by the shoulders, her tummy still pressed against Jem's. "Yeah, real good. I'm glad you're feeling better." Her voice broke and she pulled Jem back in for another prolonged hug. "Sorry, it's all these pregnancy hormones."

After a slightly weepy start from Rita, spirits lifted as the food arrived and, for most of them, the alcohol went down. The slow Tuesday evening in the restaurant was lifted by lively chatter and banter between the siblings. However, not long after the last bite was consumed and the clank of cutlery died down Mike and Rita made their escape.

"Sorry Jem, it's this bloody indigestion. It's keeping me up half of the night, I'm absolutely exhausted. Honestly, if I didn't know any better I'd tell this little one to get a move on so I can get some sleep!" Rita exclaimed as she rhythmically ran a hand across the top of her pregnant belly. "I'll see you tomorrow though, for lunch right?"

"You betcha! Do you need me to fetch anything?"

"No food, but don't forget that left over tin of yellow paint. I wanted to finish decorating the baby's room."

"No worries."

After exchanging a quick farewell the couple retreated, leaving Jem and Lucy to share a final drink with Linda and her husband before they too turned in for the evening.

***

Jem awoke to the weak spring sun filtering through the light curtains in the bedroom. She'd booked off the next 4 days, working extra shifts so that she could stack up some free days to relax and help Rita with the finishing touches on the nursery, ready for when the baby was due to arrive in the next couple of weeks. Determined to maintain her good mood Jem leapt out of bed and busied herself with the coffee machine before scanning on-line shopping sites for the perfect present, in preparation for the new arrival. By 10.30am, after far too much shopping had been done and far too much coffee had been consumed, Jem checked in on Lucy at the shop before taking the long way round to Rita and Mike's.

The scenic path lead her through a small wooded area, over a stream, which although still partially frozen now had a steady flow of clear melt water cutting a path through the opaque ice. Jem took a deep breath and released it in a cloud of condensation around her. The late February day was cold, and despite some signs of spring peeking through the snowy embankments, it was still bracing and engulfed in a crisp layer of white.

Jem concentrated on the sounds of countryside around her; the crunching of her boots through the snow, the shrill chirping and high pitched calls of birds busying themselves with the deeds of spring, the rattle of her slightly laboured breathing and the gentle trickle and burbling of water along its course that was never too far away. It all played as a healthy distraction from her wayward thoughts which echoed with the light chuckle, amusing word choice, gentle curves and throaty moans of the blonde that haunted her dreams. *'Damn'*.

By the time Jem arrived at Rita's her cheeks were flush from the crisp cool wind and the healthy pace at which she had traversed the snowy route.

"Hello!" Jem called from the back door as she placed the tin of summer yellow paint on the kitchen worktop and proceeded to remove her heavy snow boots. Once her snow encrusted footwear had been stowed on the shoe rack Jem called again, realising she was an hour early for their lunch date. "Hellooooo!"

A muffled sound from upstairs caught Jem's attention and she began to ascend the stairs two at a time. "Rita, it's me. I'm early. Are you okay?"

"Jem…I'm in the nursery." Rita sounded odd, which spurred Jem to move a little quicker up the stairs.

Jem pushed open the waxed oak door into the bright, freshly painted room to find Rita lent over the crib, a puddle at her feet. "Hey, how you doing?" Jem asked in a soft tone as she crossed the threshold.

"Arrgghhh…I'm really glad you're early." Rita squeezed the wooden railing and bent lower. "Oooohhh." Talking gave way to panting for several moments before she eventually resumed in a slightly breathless, stilted voice. "Dammit, this hurts Jem."

"Okay. When did they start?" Jen soothed as she checked her watch and began rubbing in circles along Rita's lower back.

"I'm not sure." Rita tried to straighten but immediately doubled back over in pain. "I can't straighten up long enough to see the clock…or even get to the phone."

"It's okay. I'm here now." Jem extended her motions, running the palm of one hand up and down the full length of Rita's back with while she typed out a text to Mike. "Did Mike go to that meeting in Bloomsville?"

Rita lifted her cheek onto her forearm and peered at Jem. "Yeah. I was okay this morning, just a bit of indigestion, but I've been struggling with that for days."

"Okay. I've texted him…How you feeling now?"

"A bit better now you're here." She said honestly.

Jem tucked a strand of loose hair behind Rita's ear and looked at her critically. She was a little pale, apart from the flush to her cheeks and up her neck. Her waters had clearly broken at some point while she'd been stood at the crib, but it looked clear which was a relief to Jem. "Okay. I think we should get you out of those soggy leggings and socks. Maybe into the bedroom?"

Rita nodded, but as she shifted to leave her position by the crib another contraction set in. She grabbed Jem by the forearm and squeezed as she groaned and panted through the pain. Glancing sideways at her watch Jem calculated that only 6 minutes had passed since the last contraction. '*Shit*'.

After a minute or so Rita recovered and Jem led her slowly to the en-suite where she helped her pregnant sister-in-law strip off the soggy bottoms, then collected the bathrobe from the hook on the back of the door. She helped Rita shrug it over her shoulders and then pulled the front closed, in an attempt to give her some semblance of privacy, although she knew that would probably all go out of the window if the labour progressed.

"Do you want to lie on the bed? I'm just going to get a couple of things from downstairs. Would you like a drink? Hot water bottle?"

"Yes and yes!" Rita positioned herself against the headboard while Jem adjusted the pillows. Once she was settled Jem raced downstairs, the phone attached to her ear.

The phone rung out and Jem spoke in a voice that belied the urgency she felt. The last thing she wanted was Mike getting panicked and driving like a madman. "Mike. Just to let you know, you need to set off home. The sooner the better, please. Thank you."

Jem rummaged through the cupboard under the sink, emerging with the first aid kit she'd given them as a house warming gift, before flying back up the stairs. As she entered the bedroom Rita was writhing on the bed, clumps of duvet fisted in each hand as she rode out another contraction.

"Okay, Rita. I'm gonna phone for the ambulance."

Jem made the call as she scrubbed her hands in the bathroom. After relaying the facts and the address it was on its way. Jem perched on the side of the bed and clasped Rita's left hand, before smoothing the wavy auburn hair off her sweaty brow. "Okay honey, the ambulance is on its way. How we doing?"

"Oh my God Jem. It hurts!...I think the baby's coming!"

Jem could hear the panic in Rita's voice and continued to stroke her hair in an attempt to soothe her. "Hey, I'm here. Nothing to worry about. I'll look after you. Mike's on his way and the ambulance will be here any minute." Again, Jem kept her voice low and steady, this was part of the professional façade she knew was vital to maintain a sense of calm. *'Okay, so a few white lies, but she doesn't need to know that Mike's not answering and the ambulance will be another 25 minutes. Eeeek!'*

Rita gripped Jem's hand with a force strong enough to grind the bones together and cause Jem to clench her teeth in order to stop the yelp of pain that was desperate to escape. "AAARRRGGGHHH!...Jem I need to push!"

"NO! Breathe through it. Pant. Hah, hah, hah." Jem demonstrated, trying to get Rita to copy. Once the contraction subsided Rita laid back limply. All the exertion clearly starting to take its toll. Jem took the opportunity to don some latex gloves and risk a peek at the business end. "Rita. Do you mind if we have a little look to see what's going on?"

Rita shook her head, her legs were already spread wide from the natural instinct to push. As Jem untangled the robe she could see the crown of the baby's head. This baby was coming whether we were ready or not. *'Fuck!'*

The next 10 minutes passed in a blur of contractions, pushing, grunting, shouting and eventually the high pitched cry of a new set of lungs.

"It's a boy!" Jem called, emotion thickening her voice. She cut and tied the cord then gently wrapped him in a soft brushed cotton sheet, assessing his colour and counting his fingers and toes as she prepared to hand him over to Rita who, although exhausted, managed a watery smile as the tears streamed down her cheeks.

Jem carefully transferred the precious bundle into the mothers waiting arms. "Hi!" Rita whispered as she administered her first tender kiss.

The calmness of the moment was a stark contrast to those they had just shared minutes ago and the sudden change in atmosphere was overwhelming. Jem struggled with the tenuous hold on her emotions, the joy of a new baby and relief that he had arrived safely.

A huge bang and then the thumping of heavy, clumsy feet on the runs of the stairs invaded the peace that had settled in the bedroom. Just a moment later and a very flustered looking Mike burst through the door. His tie was askew and his hair was on end where he had run his hands frantically through it. He stopped dead in the doorway, his eyes pinned on Rita and the bundle in her arms. As if in slow motion he stumbled forwards and fell onto his knees beside his wife and son, looking in awe before planting the softest kiss onto the new-born's head and then onto his wife's lips. "I love you." *'There goes the dam!'* Jem managed before the well of tears stored in her eyes broke free in a silent river down her cheeks.

Chapter 19

Rachel pulled up in front of the store. Much to her surprise a 'closed' sign was posted on the door with a hastily scrawled note. 'It's a boy!' *'Oh wow, I wonder if he arrived on Jem's birthday?'* Rachel considered as she made her way back to 'The Beast', where she retrieved the A4 envelope before proceeding up the corrugated metal stairs at the back of the shop to Jem's apartment. Her chunky Cat boots clanked and echoed loudly as she climbed.

At the top she hesitated, absently weighing and transferring the thick manila envelope from one had to the other. After procrastinating for a few moments she shook herself into action. *'You don't want to be caught loitering by Jem, do you?'* Rather than knocking Rachel pushed the envelope through the narrow gap under the door and left.

***

Jem pulled up onto the drive way, the engine still running as she gave Lucy a half embrace and a quick peck on the cheek. The elderly lady gingerly exited the car and paced up the path to the front door. Once Lucy was safely inside, Jem manoeuvred back down the drive and through the quiet streets to her apartment. She was beat. The excitement of delivering her first baby, her nephew no less, then all the kerfuffle of getting across to the hospital had taken its toll. On the drive home she felt the adrenaline wear off and had to open the window to keep her eyes from drooping in front of the wheel.

Opening the bright green door to her little flat, she realised there was something caught underneath it. *'An envelope. Huh?'* Jem placed it on the small wooden dining table before she began the strip tease to the shower. *'The quicker I'm clean, the sooner I'll be in bed!'*

***

Jem strolled along the path which meandered around the snow laden pines down to where the babble of a small brook got louder before the glint of sunlight, reflecting off the water, came into view. Fergal's Creek was one of Rachel's favourite places. As the path widened around the water Jem felt a warm hand grasp her own and looked up to see Rachel's face illuminated by the mellow spring sunshine. Rachel leaned into her shoulder and rested her head in the crook of Jem's neck as they continued around the creek, stopping every now and again to point out animal prints in the snow. They even spied a family of deer, who looked up, as if caught in a headlight before dashing away through the trees and out of sight. Eventually the tall pines thinned out and the path began winding up towards Rachel's cabin.

As they reached the front door Jem was suddenly transported to the foot of her bed. Rachel had transformed out of her warm winter clothes and was now dressed in a dusky rose, clingy silk negligée. Her blonde hair fell in waves across her shoulders, soft pink lips that begged to be kissed, parted and glistened in the low lamplight that cast shadows across her face and the underside of her chest. *'Hold on, wasn't it daytime?'*

"You look so beautiful." Rachel leant into Jem's touch and closed her eyes. Jem brushed her lips softly across her bruised cheek and breathed "I love you" into her ear. *'It wasn't bruised before was it?'* Jem's befuddled brain briefly considered before she was pulled back into the scene.

168

Very tentatively Rachel closed the distance between their bodies and placed a slow, lingering kiss on Jem's mouth. Jem made no move to deepen their contact and after a beat Rachel took the initiative, sweeping her tongue across Jem's lips which instantly opened, allowing their tongues to tangle and move against each other sensually. Jem kept her hands on Rachel's hips while Rachel's hands reacquainted themselves with as much of Jem's body as possible, eventually finding their way under her soft cotton top to caress the warm flesh beneath.

Jem obediently followed Rachel's instruction, lifting her arms up as Rachel pulled the hem of the loose t-shirt she wore to bed up over her head. Once removed Rachel held Jem's gaze as she ran her hands up the toned tummy, around her back and unhooked her bra. As this fell to the ground Rachel smoothed her hands over the pale flesh, rubbing her thumbs rhythmically over Jem's nipples, which had hardened into firm peaks. Breaking eye contact, Rachel lent forward and took one of the firm peaks into her mouth while gently kneading the underside of each breast. Jem released a soft moan, which fuelled Rachel to untie the bow at the front of Jem's soft, brushed cotton, tartan pyjama bottoms and then push them down her hips. One hand gripped a firm buttock and the other slipped down the front of her panties, into the wet heat waiting for her.

The plethora of sensation from the suckling of her breast, kneading of her backside and the penetration of Rachel's fingers made her legs shake and she very gingerly laid her hands on Rachel's shoulders. Rachel sunk to her knees and kissed her way down Jem's abdomen, tugging her knickers down her thighs and then placing a soft kiss on the landing strip of curls that she had revealed. Rachel pulled away slightly and looked up at Jem whose yes were hooded, she silently beckoned Rachel up by holding out her arms, but Rachel simply shook her head and gently pushed Jem by her hips onto the bed and spread her legs wide.

"Rachel?" Jem pleaded, but Rachel simply looked at her with glassy eyes, moved closer and then kissed her way from her knee, up her inner thigh to her sex. Jem took a sharp intake of breath as she fell backwards onto the bed. Rachel explored slowly, mapping out Jem's most intimate area with her tongue, both hands gripping firmly onto her legs. With each stroke of her tongue and sighed moan from Jem, she increased the pressure. Jem began to move uncontrollably until Rachel stopped abruptly, sat up and held her head at an unnatural angle, her eyes blank and unfocussed. "Bbbrrrrrppppp".

"You're not for me!" Rachel whispered. Rachel's face suddenly fell and hardened and she wrapped her arms around the oversized baby blue shirt she was now wearing. "YOU'RE NOT bbbrrrrrppppp FOR ME! Bbbrrrrrppppp." She yelled.

'Shit!'

The unfamiliar sound her new phone ringing finally filtered Jem consciousness and ripped her from the dream. Jem sat bolt upright and immediately started fumbling in a panic for the small devise that was flashing brightly, making a God awful sound and vibrating like it was having a tantrum on the bedside table.

"'Lo." Jem mumbled, still tugging the thick mop of hair from across her eyes.

"Good morning Jem dear."

"Gram?! What's up?" Jem asked in a panic.

"Oh nothing honey. Did I wake you?"

"Um, yeah." Jem rubbed the sleep from one of her eyes. "What time is it?"

"10.30am. Sorry, I thought you'd be up by now."

"S'okay." Jem lied, sure that the dream would have ended differently if she hadn't been rudely interrupted by the stupid phone.

"Did you see the news? Oh no, of course not! Well...Rachel's been busy...sold a painting. You might want to have a look."

"Yeah, okay, whatever." Jem huffed until Lucy stopped her mid mumble.

"Now that's enough Jemima. Get out of bed and stop wallowing. I want to see you happy and whatever you're doing at the moment is not working. You will get out of bed, put on the news and go visit your friend up at the cabin. She's back in town and it's about time you two talked." And with that Lucy ended the call.

Jem looked perplexed at the blank screen. "I've just been told off...I'm 31 years of age and I've been told off...What do you mean wallowing? I've turned over a new leaf for Christ's sake!" Jem mumbled grumpily as she hoicked herself out of bed and padded across the polished wood floor to the bathroom.

Once she'd finished in the bathroom Jem flipped on the TV as she made her way to the kitchen to brew some coffee. As she passed the small dining table she noticed the thick brown envelope from last night. A bold cursive 'Jem' was all it had on it. Jem began fingering it open as one of the news headlines caught her attention.

"And finally, reclusive artist L R Davies has surprised us again." The smooth, deep voice of the male news reporter explained. "The generous but anonymous artist, famous for donating monies raised from the sales of his, or her, artwork to the children's charity ACC, has 'wowed' the art world with the surprise auction of a new piece. Although not the artist's usual style, it did little to deter the bidders. In fact, there was a lengthy bidding war at the famous auction house, Christie's. The piece, simply named 'The One' sold

171

for a whopping $7.2 million. The reclusive artist even penned a brief letter stating that the money was to be shared 3 ways with ACC, Victim Support Services and the American Heart Association. But that's not the most unusual part, right Cassie?"

"That's right Bruce. The extremely secretive artist revealed that this piece was actually a dedication to, and I quote, 'someone I love, but hurt. I hope you can forgive me. I will love you always.'" Cassie turned expectantly to her co-host who picked up the cue.

"Wow, what a powerful message. Well I hope everything works out, we'll have to keep our eyes on the next pieces to give us some clues. Right, now onto the weather. Charlotte, what does the day have in store for us?"

Jem blinked at the screen, which panned away from the perfectly coiffed and tanned presenters that were sat in front of a large image of an oil portrait of a very familiar face, to the smiley and rather overenthusiastic weather reporter. Remembering the thick envelope in her hand Jem hastily tore it open to reveal a Christie's brochure with a pink post-it note protruding from inside. A card fluttered to the floor. Jem picked this up and began reading the same bold, cursive handwriting from the front of the envelope.

Dear Jem,

Happy Birthday

I don't know if you can ever forgive my obscene behaviour. I did it because I love you and didn't want the press or the public to ever hurt you, like they have me. I was frightened and foolish. These last 2 months have been difficult and I have come to realise that I don't want to lose you from my life, even if you only want to be friends. I hope you can forgive me.

I wanted to dedicate my most recent piece to you on your birthday.

Happy birthday

All my love

Rachel xoxo

Jem stood in the kitchen, hair tussled, her feet bare and her mind completely blank. *'What do I do with that?'*

Chapter 20

"Rachel, where do you want me to put this?" James called from the kitchen.

"Errr, just shove it in the miscellaneous box and I'll deal with it once we've moved." Rachel's muffled voice called from behind the thick curtains she was unhooking from their rail along the top of the patio windows.

"I'll get it!"

"What?!" Rachel exclaimed as she staggered behind the curtain, gathering the thick material in her arms as she released the last hook.

"The door." James chuckled. "I'll get it." He checked the peep hole before opening the door. "Hi, can I help you?"

"Oh, errr, hi. I was just looking for Rachel. Is she in?"

"Of course, please come in." James stepped back and Jem stiffly and rather self-consciously entered the cabin. "Rachel, Jem's here to see you."

Jem's head snapped up to look into the face of the tall man with a sandy mop of hair. '*How did he know my name?*' He had a young looking face and a genuine smile that reached his pale blue eyes. The sudden clatter and thud of the heavy lounge curtains being dropped drew Jem's eye into the sitting area where Rachel stood stock still, a pile of material at her feet.

Jem took in a lungful of air, ran her sweaty palms down her thighs and then shakily released her breath. "Hi Rachel." '*God, she's stunning.*'

James looked back and forth between the women before interrupting the short silence that had started between them. "I'm going down to the store and then up to Wilf's. Do you need anything Rachel?"

Rachel dragged her eyes momentarily away from Jem to address James. "No thank you."

James nodded his acknowledgment, grabbed some car keys off the side and quickly disappeared from the cabin. Jem and Rachel continued to stand quietly observing each other until Rachel finally gave a gentle smile and welcomed her guest. "Hi Jem. It's good to see you."

Jem nodded, her features seemingly too paralysed to generate a smile. Seeing Rachel in the flesh had taken her by surprise, even though she'd had more than enough time to prepare herself for this moment. "You too." The whole scene felt surreal and awkward. Jem stuffed her hands into the pocket of her down jacket and looked down at her shoes. They were muddy and covered in snow from the walk up the lane to the cabin. Upon realising the mess she was making she walked back to the door and onto the thick welcome mat.

Rachel jumped into action. "Please...don't go!" She ran to Jem but suddenly stopped short of reaching for her. "I had hoped we could at least talk?" She wrapped her arms protectively around herself, the baggy sleeves on the cream, heavy knit jumper almost covering her hands.

"Sorry...my boots." Jem pointed at her muddy boots and Rachel blushed before nodding her head.

"Can I get you a cup of tea or coffee? I don't think that's been packed away yet."

"Sure. Why are you packing? Are you moving in? With him?" Jem couldn't stop the question as it spilled from her lips. '*Jealous much?*'

"What!" Rachel's head whipped sideways to look at Jem, the kettle dangling limply from one hand. "No, of course not…Sorry. I haven't explained anything, have I?" Rachel filled the kettle and set it on the stove before leaning her back against it. "That's James. He my new PA slash personal protector."

"Oh."

"After all that stuff before Christmas I realised a few things…I wasn't managing my personal affairs very well and I have put myself, at times, in danger or difficult positions by not allowing or accepting help." Rachel turned away from Jem as the kettle whistled and poured the steaming water into 2 cups.

Jem moved back into the cabin in her stockinged feet and took a seat at the dining table as Rachel placed a mug in front of her. Rachel took the seat opposite and continued, spurred on by Jem's silence. "So…I am moving…but only up to Wilf's cabin." She quickly finished. "I bought Wilf's and I'm going to expand this place, well, rebuild it really so that it can become my main residence…I'm leaving LA, but I'll keep a residence there for any time I need to visit for filming or whatever." Rachel took a sip of the scalding liquid and looked at Jem over the rim of her mug. Jem's lean figure was slightly hunched forward as both hands gripped the mug, her gaze firmly set on the dark liquid and her features revealing little of what she was thinking. Rachel could feel the panic rising in her chest. '*Why would Jem trust me, I told her I didn't want her for God's sake. Maybe she didn't get the letter?*' "Did you get my card?"

Jem looked up from her cup and focussed on Rachel's. "Yes, thank you…I…I didn't know what to make of it really." Jem responded quietly before letting out a long sigh. Rachel felt her heart sink. "These last 2 months have been pretty rough for me too. I thought I was just getting myself together, ya know?"

A lone tear escaped and travelled down Rachel's cheek as she nodded her understanding. "I'm so sorry Jem. I'm sorry I hurt you. I just…I just didn't realise what it was like to be in love."

Jem looked up and upon seeing the tears traversing Rachel's face, she unwrapped a hand from the mug and reached across the table to cup Rachel's face, rubbing the tears away with the pad of her thumb. Rachel pounced on the opportunity and laid her hand over Jem's, repositioning it so that she could kiss the soft palm before entwining their fingers.

Jem didn't resist so Rachel extended the contact, raising her other hand to tenderly trace her fingertips along Jem's jaw, up the side of her face and then up to tuck a loose strand of soft, brown hair behind her ear. But the table was in the way, so very slowly, fingers still entwined with Jem's she slipped from her chair, onto her knees in front of Jem, who swivelled slightly in her seat to face Rachel. Rachel released Jem's hand and placed her palms flat onto Jem's thighs as she lifted her face towards Jem's.

"I love you…Please…please forgive me?" Rachel leant forward, parting Jem's legs so she could shuffle forward and reach her mouth. She placed a feather light kiss onto Jem's lips. When Jem didn't retreat she leaned closer and pressed her lips more firmly against Jem's. Jem accepted, her hands reaching round to hold Rachel's head in place as she deepened the kiss.

What started as tender soon escalated as lips and tongues moved more frantically against each other. Rachel ran her palms up Jem's denim clad legs, her thumbs tracing the inseam, before journeying around her waist to hold her in a tight embrace, the thick down jacket hindering any further intimate contact. As the urgency ebbed, the tenderness returned before both women gently pulled away. Rachel blinked at the blinding desire that had taken over her. Her core throbbed and her breast ached. "I love you…please, please say you'll forgive me."

Before Jem could respond there was a loud rap on the door, effectively breaking the spell they had fallen under. Rachel hurried to her feet and crossed the room. Before opening the door she spied at the visitor through the peep hole. "Sorry." She directed at Jem before opening the door. "Hi."

"Hi Rachel." A smart gentleman in a shirt and tie beneath a warm woollen jacket reached forward and he and Rachel shook hands. "This is David, the contractor." He moved aside and introduced Rachel to the builder, who was dressed more informally in blue jeans and a plaid shirt. David lent forward and they shook hands too.

"Please come in. Sorry, James has just popped out. But I'll give him a quick call now so we can go ahead with our meeting. Please take a seat and I'll grab you a drink. Would you like a tea or coffee?"

Once she'd taken their order she walked back through to the kitchen, where Jem was putting on her boots. "I'm sorry. It's the architect and contractor about the renovation. James must have forgotten." As soon as she'd said those words there was a loud knock, followed by James, who cautiously entered the open plan cabin.

"Sorry." He held his hands up in surrender. He gave the gentlemen a small nod and then crossed the room to Rachel. "What do you need me to do boss?"

"Could you just get them 2 coffees. I'm just going to see Jem out."

'*That's my* cue' Jem thought as she stood, straightened her jacket and walked lightly toward the door, hoping not to leave a trail of mud in her wake. Once outside, Rachel pulled the door too and stepped out onto the porch with Jem, looking around the drive. "Where are you parked?"

"Just on the bottom road. I wanted to walk up through Fergal's Creek, it's such a pretty route."

Rachel nodded. "Can I see you again?"

Jem turned to face Rachel and nodded. "I think that would be a good idea. We should talk. Maybe we could meet at Linda's or something."

"Okay. Tonight?"

"Yep, okay. Could we meet a bit later? I want to see Rita in hospital."

"Oh my goodness, yes. Please pass on my congratulations. Do we have a name yet?"

"I think they're going to announce that tonight when Gram and I go to visit."

"Okay, so Linda's at, what, 8pm?"

"Okay. See you soon." Before Jem could make her escape Rachel leaned forward and pressed a small kiss to her cheek.

"See you later."

Chapter 21

Jem rocked gently and laid a soft kiss on the shock of black hair. The little bundle yawned and made little lapping noises as he rummaged for his thumb. Jem was smitten. A wide beaming smile was plastered across her face as she took in the tiny features of the baby in her arms.

"Okay, so I really need to know a name. Speedy doesn't feel right anymore."

Rita and Mike laughed. "Okay." Mike reached for the boy and after a little awkward shimmying and shuffling to transfer the precious bundle between them he sat down next to his wife on the bed. "I would like to formally introduce you to Albert Jeremiah Shaw." At the continued hush in the room Mike looked up to see the glistening eyes of his grandmother and sister. "Well, what do you think?"

Lucy cleared her throat. "I think it's wonderful dear. Your grandfather would be so proud to have someone so special named after him." She swiped a tear from the corner of her eye and then laid her hand on Jem's forearm. "…and I think this one earned that middle name!"

"Well, we did promise that if you delivered our first born we'd name him after you! We weren't sure what the male version of Jemima was, but decided Jeremiah was pretty close."

***

After the surprisingly emotional visit at the hospital Jem arrived home keen to get in the shower. It wasn't only because Albert had been a little sick across her shoulder, but simply the weight of the day. She really wanted to cleanse herself, to have a fresh start before the next emotional whirlwind that was undoubtedly going to be her 'meeting' with Rachel.

Although they'd kissed earlier, something Jem had chastised herself for but knew she would have done it again in a heartbeat, she needed to understand where she stood. Rachel was an A-list celebrity who did photo shoots for trendy fashion mags, was a lead, award winning actress in movies set all around the world and had a secret double-life as a multi-million dollar artist. When on earth would she have time for a relationship, and that's not even factoring in the lesbian bit of that. Jem knew all of the furore around Matt's outing and, to be quite frank, thought Rachel would not want any of that kind of attention, especially after just shaking the limelight following the horrendous kidnapping by the psychopath stalker.

Jem was just stepping out of the shower when she heard a knock at the door. Looking at the clock she realised she was running late. *'Shit, I must have spent longer in the shower than I thought.'* Jem threw on a bathrobe before opening the door. Rachel stood at the top of the stairs, a small wrapped box in her hand. She wore a fitted black shirt, unbuttoned at the top to provide a tasteful hint of cleavage and a fitted black skirt. Thick stockings protected her legs from the cold and her feet were encased in practical, yet sexy, black cowboy boots. "Hi!" Jem opened the door wide to invite her in. "Sorry, I'm running late."

"It's okay. I had a drink with Linda and then thought I'd better check I'd got the right day."

"No, it's the right day. Albert puked on my shoulder and I thought I had enough time for the shower, seems I lost track a bit." Jem apologised.

"Albert, that's a lovely name. Is that after your Grandfather?"

"Yeah." Jem smiled proudly, but held back from revealing his middle name and the reasoning behind it. "Can I get you a drink while I get dressed?"

"I can get it. What would you like?"

"Errr, I've got a bottle of white wine in the fridge. I'll have a glass of that if you'll have one too?"

"Of course, go get dressed. I'll see you in a few."

Jem hastily dressed and then haphazardly blew the hairdryer across her brunette locks. It wasn't the look she was really going for, but windswept it was going to have to be! In record time Jem emerged from the bedroom.

Rachel looked up from her place on the sofa as Jem emerged from the bedroom. Her hair fell in natural loose brown curls and her make-up free face was slightly flushed. She'd clearly rushed, but looked stunning in the fitted black jeans, red high heels and matching fitted long length cashmere top. Rachel ran her eyes up Jem's form and smiled, trying not to be obvious as she letched at the gorgeous woman before her. Clearly it didn't work because Jem's cheeks heated further, turning them an even brighter shade of red. "You look lovely Jem."

"Thank you. You do too." Jem returned, slightly awkwardly.

"Here, I poured you a glass of wine." Jem sat at the opposite end of the couch to Rachel, a healthy expanse of worn leather between them. "Would you like to open your present before we go to the restaurant?" Rachel asked as she sipped from her small glass of wine.

"You know that is too kind. You didn't need to get me a gift." *'Plus, I think I already got it.'* Jem thought silently but wasn't brave enough to say out loud.

"Don't be silly, giving gifts is the best bit about Christmas and birthdays. I love watching people open their presents. I just hope you like it."

Jem gently teased off the birthday string and bow, before carefully untucking the gift wrap from the sticky tape without tearing it and unfolded the paper to reveal a black velvet box. Rachel fidgeted with her wine glass, clearly itching to rip the paper off the small box herself. Jem set the paper to one side before prying open the sprung lid. Jem's eyes widened and she smiled brightly as her gift was revealed. "Oh Rachel, that's gorgeous, thank you." Jem removed the small puffin brooch from its miniature pillow and admired it. "I'm surprised you remembered."

"Well, being from Britain the puffin isn't quite so unusual. I remember you telling me about your trip to Maine. I never knew there were puffins all the way over here…I guess it struck a chord." Rachel shrugged lightly as Jem lent over to give her a quick hug.

"Thank you. That's incredibly thoughtful."

"You're welcome." Rachel finished off the last mouthful of wine and stood. "Do you still want to go out to dinner? I said to Linda I'd let her know, but it's getting kind of late and I wouldn't want her keeping the food service open for no need."

"Of course, let's go."

Dinner went surprisingly well. Rachel was totally mesmerised by Jem's retelling of Albert's arrival and Jem asked about the new cabin and future plans for Wilf's place. As Rachel disappeared into the bathroom she reflected on the evening. '*We've avoided all the difficult and sore topics, which to be honest was the main reason why we'd agreed to meet in the first place, wasn't it?*' Either way the meeting with Rachel had reminded Jem how much she enjoyed her company.

Jem had noticed that Rachel had been careful to avoid the friendly touches she was prone to and Jem in return had focussed on her left ear! Jem chuckled at herself, Rachel was probably checking to see if there was something wrong with it, which of course there wasn't, but it was a little less enticing than looking into the depths of those true blue eyes or at the plump pink lips that Jem had difficulty resisting.

"Hey." Rachel touched Jem lightly on the shoulder to catch her attention.

"Sorry, I must have been miles away. What did you say?"

"I said we'd better get going and let Linda go to bed."

"Right." Jem stood and they both pulled on their jackets.

"Night Linda!" The two women called in unison to the back of the bar where Linda was leant over a recipe book with the chef.

"Night girls. See you at Tuesday Club?"

Jem nodded to Linda and then they made their way to the door. As they stepped into the cold night air Jem inquired "Where are you parked?"

"The Beast is at the back of yours. I thought if I wanted a drink I could leave it there and James could come and get me."

"Oh…does he not mind coming out at all hours of the night?" Jem asked, curious for an insight into Rachel's nocturnal activities.

"I wouldn't know, I'm not much of a diva, I've never had to ask him in the 6 weeks he's worked for me!" Rachel chuckled as she hooked her arm around Jem's, providing an anchor as they negotiated a patch of ice. Jem was wearing 2½ inch heels, which levelled her in height with Rachel, but weren't the most practical choice of footwear for the late February evening.

184

They walked the remainder of the way in silence. The evening was still and brisk, with a clear sky that revealed a multitude of stars above them. As they arrived at the hilariously macho truck Rachel paused. "It's been lovely tonight, but I think we pretty much avoided all the tough stuff." Rachel fiddled with an earring before removing it and placing it into her pocket. "It's like this afternoon didn't happen." She fiddled with the other earring and removed that one too. "I don't…" she let out a heavy sigh. "…I don't know what you want." She said as she began twisting the ring on her right hand. "But if it's just friendship then I'll understand, but I want you to know that I'm serious about moving here. I'm serious about what I said earlier in the letter and the card…and at the cabin…and although I fucked up…well I wasn't in a good place. Things are better now. I've had some help and I've sorted through a lot of stuff, both physical and emotional. I know what I want…and that's you." She added in a soft whisper as her eyes went from the ring she was nervously twisting to the Jem's chocolate brown eyes.

Jem studied Rachel carefully as she formulated her answer. As she was about to respond Rachel touched her lips with her fingers, effectively silencing her. "It's okay, you don't need to answer now, I understand, it's a lot to take in. Just, when you know, let me know." Rachel removed her fingers and placed a friendly kiss on her cheek. "Night."

***

Jem tossed and turned in bed, sleep evading her until eventually in the wee hours of the morning she got out of bed and made a cup of tea. She smiled at the steaming cup as she leant against the kitchen worktop. She'd never been much of a tea drinker until Rachel had introduced it at a new, entirely British, level of consumption. As she took a sip she thought about the events of the last few days.

Baby safely delivered. Check.

Massive public display of affection. Check.

Told me she loves me. Check, check and check, check, check. Really...5 times! Wow. How many times have I said it?

Jem racked her brain and replayed the last few days. *No, not once...what about before?* The scene in Lucy's spare bedroom unfolded before her eyes.

"Is this what you really want?"

Rachel shook her head while she softly answered "Yes."

"Are you sure you want this Rachel?"

Rachel cried and the tears tracked across her angry, swollen and scabbed cheek. Yes!

"What if I love you?" Ahhh, there I said it...sort of.

"Then you'd better stop. I'm not for you Jem." Rachel looked away...she looked away!

Jem stood up abruptly, the tea swirl perilously close to the rim of the cup. *'I'm the biggest fool, ever!'* Jem slammed the cup down on the counter, the contents finally escaping their confines to puddle and then pour in little rivulets off the counter. Jem ignored the stream of tea and ran into the bedroom where she threw on a pair of jeans, a sweater and slid her bare feet into the nearest pair of snow boots.

***

The crunch of tyres on the gravel drive caused Rachel to pause, mid stroke of the pallet knife, and saunter over to the kitchen window which felt bare and naked without its blind. Rachel could see the door open on the familiar red SUV and even in the dark she could make out Jem's figure hurrying towards the cabin. She laid down the wooden palette, thick with oils ready to be applied to the board, on the kitchen worktop and opened the door before Jem reached it.

"What are you doing up, scurrying around in the dark?" Rachel asked as Jem climbed the wooden porch stairs.

Jem slowed as she reached the top step and looked at Rachel as she answered. "I couldn't sleep. What are you doing up?"

Rachel shrugged. "I couldn't sleep either. I do a lot of painting at night." Rachel looked at Jem who was now leant in the doorway, the tails of a night shirt peeking out from under her down jacket. "Did you want to come in or were you just out for a midnight stroll?"

Jem straightened, looked Rachel in the eye and then reached forward to grasp her warm hands in her own ice cold ones. A shiver travelled up Rachel's spine.

"You told me I should tell you when I know." Jem slowly leant forward until her lips were just an inch from Rachel's and whispered. "I know…I love you." Jem closed the gap, her cold lips revelling in the warm softness of Rachel's. Jem released her hands and gripped her around the waist, removing all space between their bodies as their kiss deepened. Rachel abruptly halted the kiss, delivered a smouldering look and tugged Jem into the cabin.

About the Author

C Mack is based in the beautiful Yorkshire Dales, England. A teacher by day, in the evening she dotes on her children and wrestles with a menagerie of pets before she can finally settle into her battered writing chair or curl up in front of the fire where she loves to sink into a good book.

'The Cabin' is C Mack's first novella, but be assured there are more on the way.

To see more about C Mack and further publications, visit her author page on Amazon at:

https://www.amazon.co.uk/C-Mack/e/B001KDGEP6/ref=sr_ntt_srch_lnk_1?qid=1487420975&sr=1-1

Or on Goodreads at:

https://www.goodreads.com/author/show/8513533.C_Mack

Printed in Great Britain
by Amazon

63658791R00113